BUZZ ~~AND~~ THE TRACK

"The first time I saw him, I thought he was one of the most drop-dead gorgeous males I'd ever seen. Not the glossy, overgroomed sort, but an 'I've lived and loved every minute of it' guy. I couldn't make myself look away."
—Sarah Stanton

"I was supposed to be talking up my vineyard. Instead, I spent my time speculating on what buttoned-up Sarah would look like with her hair down and one or two buttons undone on her short-sleeved blouse."
—Steve Clayton

"I've never seen my dad so enthralled by a woman. It's good for him, and for me. The only thing that would make me happier would be to find that lead I've been looking for on the Gina Grosso mystery."
—Mattie Clayton

"I admit I've been distracted recently by the search for my missing daughter, but even so, Sarah has become a dear friend. I'd be thrilled if she and Steve could make a relationship work."
—Patsy Grosso

DORIEN KELLY

is a former attorney who is much happier as an author. In addition to her years practicing business law, at one point or another she has also been a waitress, a bank teller and a professional chauffeur to her three children. Her current (and very romantic) day job is executive director of a lighthouse keepers association.

When Dorien isn't writing or keeping lighthouses lit, she loves to garden, travel and be with her friends and family. A RITA® Award nominee, she is also the winner of a Romance Writers of America's Golden Heart Award, a Booksellers' Best Award, a Maggie Award and a Gayle Wilson Award of Excellence. She lives in a small village in Michigan with one or more of her children, the love of her life (when he can be home) and three crazed dogs.

NASCAR

A TASTE FOR SPEED

Dorien Kelly

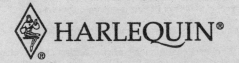

HARLEQUIN®

TORONTO • NEW YORK • LONDON
AMSTERDAM • PARIS • SYDNEY • HAMBURG
STOCKHOLM • ATHENS • TOKYO • MILAN • MADRID
PRAGUE • WARSAW • BUDAPEST • AUCKLAND

Recycling programs
for this product may
not exist in your area.

ISBN-13: 978-0-373-18528-3

A TASTE FOR SPEED

Copyright © 2009 by Harlequin Books S.A.

Dorien Kelly is acknowledged as the author of this work.

NASCAR® and the NASCAR Library Collection® are registered trademarks of the National Association for Stock Car Auto Racing, Inc.

This edition published by arrangement with Harlequin Books S.A.

® and TM are trademarks of the publisher. Trademarks indicated with ® are registered in the United States Patent and Trademark Office, the Canadian Trade Marks Office and in other countries.

www.eHarlequin.com

Printed in U.S.A.

To Erin Lee Kelly, who gets to eat out a whole lot
when Mom has a deadline.
I love you!

NASCAR HIDDEN LEGACIES

The Grossos

Dean Grosso
m.
Patsy Clark Grosso

Patsy's brother

Kent Grosso
(fiancée Tanya Wells)

Gina Grosso
(deceased)

Sophia Grosso
(fiancé Justin Murphy)

Dean's best friend

The Clarks

Andrew Clark
(divorced)

Garrett Clark ⑯
(Andrew's stepson)

Patsy's cousin

Jake McMasters ⑧

Kent's agent

Kane Ledger ⑦

The Cargills

Alan Cargill (widower)

Nathan Cargill ⑤

The Claytons

Steve Clayton ⑩

Mattie Clayton ⑭

Business partner

Damon Tieri ⑪

The Branches

Maeve Branch
(div. Hilton Branch) m.
Chuck Lawrence

Will Branch ②

Bart Branch

Penny Branch m.
Craig Lockhart

Sawyer Branch
(fiancée
Lucy Gunter)

---

① *Scandals and Secrets*
② *Black Flag, White Lies*
③ *Checkered Past*
④ *From the Outside*
⑤ *Over the Wall*
⑥ *No Holds Barred*
⑦ *One Track Mind*
⑧ *Within Striking Distance*
⑨ *Running Wide Open*
⑩ *A Taste for Speed*
⑪ *Force of Nature*
⑫ *Banking on Hope*
⑬ *The Comeback*
⑭ *Into the Corner*
⑮ *Raising the Stakes*
⑯ *Crossing the Line*

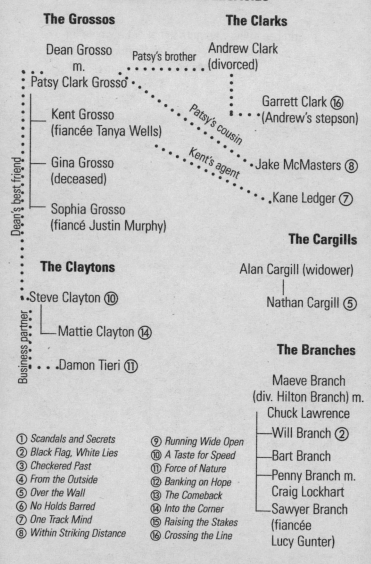

THE FAMILIES AND THE CONNECTIONS

The Sanfords

Bobby Sanford
(deceased)
m.
Kath Sanford

- Adam Sanford ①

- Brent Sanford ⑫

- Trey Sanford ⑨

The Hunts

Dan Hunt
m.
Linda (Willard) Hunt
(deceased)

- Ethan Hunt ⑥

- Jared Hunt ⑮

- Hope Hunt ⑫

- Grace Hunt Winters ⑯
(widow of Todd Winters)

The Mathesons

Brady Matheson
(widower)
(fiancée Julie-Anne Blake)

- Chad Matheson ③

- Zack Matheson ⑬

- Trent Matheson
(fiancée Kelly Greenwood)

The Daltons

Buddy Dalton
m.
Shirley Dalton

- Mallory Dalton ④

- Tara Dalton ①

- Emma-Lee Dalton

CHAPTER ONE

SARAH STANTON FELT SOMEONE watching her, and not in the semi-interested way that her undergraduate students sometimes did. This was intense, startlingly so. She glanced around the crowd milling under the festive white tent but couldn't spot the watcher. After a moment she decided that she'd probably imagined the sensation. She was jet-lagged and as far out of her usual academic element as she could imagine. The only thing a private NASCAR prerace party held in common with a college lecture hall was Sarah, herself.

The things a professor must do in the name of research...

Sarah smiled as she took in the activity around her. Last night Dean and Patsy Grosso, owners of Cargill-Grosso Racing, had flown her with them in their private jet from North Carolina to California's Sonoma Valley. In a little while she would witness her first NASCAR race. Just in time, too, since this fall she would be moving from Larchmont College's general business faculty into its motorsports management program. The Grossos were donors to that program and also active participants, inviting interns to work at Cargill-Grosso Racing. And now they'd agreed to take her on as their summer project, bringing her to races so that she could get up to speed—so to speak—before classes started.

Like many residents of the Charlotte area, Sarah appreciated what NASCAR had brought to her hometown. She hadn't been an active fan, though. Between her classes and the writing she did to stay on the tenure track, her outside amusements were few—some biking and tennis, a bit of casual dating and weekly gatherings with her colleagues.

The prickly feeling on the back of Sarah's neck had fully subsided. Amen to that, too. She rather liked her personal life below the radar. Standing at the podium while teaching was attention enough these days.

She looked to her right, where the Grossos had been detained by representatives of Smoothtone Music, hosts of this gathering, and more important, sponsor of their son Kent's car. Sarah was content to be standing at a tall café table on the outskirts of the crowd. Here she could enjoy the warm June breeze that slipped off the surrounding dusty brown hills and type notes into her PDA. The Grossos had already introduced her to so many potential program contacts that if she didn't get the information down now, it would slip away in the haze of excitement.

Suddenly that tingly feeling crept over her…and stronger this time, too. Sarah looked up from her phone's small screen, and her gaze locked with a man's. Not any man, either. Small wonder she'd tingled. He was one of the most drop-dead gorgeous males she'd ever seen. He wasn't the glossy, overgroomed sort, but more of an "I've lived and loved every minute of it" guy.

Sarah couldn't bring herself to look away. She'd bet that she wasn't the first woman to be so drawn, either. He appeared to be a handful of years—or maybe a few more—beyond her own forty-two, but he wore those years well. Very, very well.

Lucky man.

Her watcher's dark blond hair was a bit long for him to be the corporate type, and his tan spoke of a man who spent a great deal of time outdoors. A smile played about his mouth as he inclined his head in a gesture of curiosity and something more. If she were the sort to flatter herself—which, generally, she wasn't—she'd call it admiration.

"Earth to Sarah," she muttered to herself, forcing her attention away from Sonoma's answer to a Greek god. She focused on her phone, but didn't yet have the mental wherewithal to actually read what was on the screen. Until her brain reengaged, however, she would fake it, since gawking at a stranger wasn't her usual gig. In the midst of her faux note-taking, she allowed herself another glance at the handsome stranger. He gave her a full-out grin.

The unwelcome heat of color rose on her face. Honestly, she couldn't recall the last time she'd blushed. Suffice it to say that it must have been a few decades ago. And as a mature, independent woman, she knew she couldn't slip from this tent and hide, as impulse dictated. She could, however, search for her composure on the way to the wine-tasting table.

Quelling the urge to take one last look at the man, she instead pocketed her PDA, slipped into the crowd and joined a group sampling small pours of wine. Sarah selected a Chardonnay from the offerings. The wine was smooth and rich against her tongue, its taste bringing to mind both citrus and a sweet whisper of her mother's peach pie. She let her eyes slip closed as she savored the mix of flavors and the calming moment.

"There you are, Sarah," Patsy Grosso said from beside her. "I thought for a moment that we'd lost you."

Sarah smiled. "It was more a matter of my finding the wine bar."

"You're a wine lover?" Patsy asked.

Though they had met casually at a number of college fund-raising events and chatted more intimately on the cross-country flight to Sonoma, they were still in the "getting to know you" phase of friendship. And what Sarah had seen of Patsy thus far, she liked.

"Wine within my budget, without a doubt," she said to Patsy.

"All the more reason you need to meet Steve."

"Steve?"

"He's a very dear friend of the family. I think you'll enjoy him. Come on over and say hello."

"Sounds wonderful." Sarah took another sip of her Chardonnay, then fell in next to Patsy, who was already threading through the gathering.

"Quite the party, isn't it?" Patsy commented as they

paused to let a couple pass the other way. "Hang on, though. Dean and Steve are right ahead…just the other side of the sweets table," she added with a quick flick of her prettily manicured nails.

Sarah let her gaze roll past the chocolate fountain— never an easy task—to the two men Patsy had gestured at.

In this crowd, what were the odds? Apparently one hundred percent in favor of meeting Mr. Perfect…who was giving her yet another resistance-melting smile.

If Patsy hadn't been right next to her, she probably would have played coward and turned heel. As it was, she must have slowed enough to get Patsy's attention.

"Is everything okay?" Patsy asked.

"I'm fine," Sarah fibbed.

Patsy gave Sarah a perceptive look. "Steve has a way of slowing women a step. He is easy on the eyes, isn't he?"

"Not painful at all," Sarah agreed. Actually, there was something vaguely familiar about him, and not just because they'd been checking each other out. But she had no time to try to place him, because here they were.

Patsy made the introductions. "Sarah, this is Steve Clayton. Steve, this is Sarah Stanton, a new friend of ours."

He offered his hand, and after switching her wine-glass into her left hand, she took it. His grip was warm and firm. While her brain prompted her to be business-like, every other cell of her body relished the moment.

"Hello, Sarah. It's a pleasure to finally meet you."

"Finally?" Patsy asked, but all Steve gave her in response was a crooked smile and a shrug. And Sarah couldn't seem to pull her attention from Steve. What would she have said, anyway? "We've been staring at each other like two teenagers" didn't seem a very dignified response.

"Enjoying the Chardonnay?" he asked Sarah, then released her palm.

"Very much."

"Good. It's mine."

"Yours?" For one endless instant, she wondered if she'd somehow ended up with his glass. Then she managed to put his words into context. "Wait...you own the vineyard?"

"I do."

"Wow! How wonderful! That must be an amazing job."

Now that she had some more information, she wracked her brain for where she'd seen him before. Maybe she'd seen his picture in one of her wine or food magazines?

"It's a challenge," he said. "And there's nothing better than a good challenge." The glint in his blue eyes let her know that she wasn't mistaken in reading another level of meaning into his words.

She took a final sip of the small tasting pour of wine she'd received. "Very true."

"You'll have to visit Pebble Valley while you're out here," he said. "Our new tasting room opened this past spring. I think you'd enjoy it."

"I'd love to, but this is a quick trip for me," she said.

"We're introducing Sarah to the world of NASCAR," Patsy said.

"For work or pleasure?" he asked Sarah.

"I think life is best when both combine, don't you?" she replied.

His smile grew. "Absolutely. I've lived my life doing just that."

"This is work for me, in a way. In the fall I'm joining the motorsports management faculty at the college where I teach. I'd feel a fraud teaching racing management without first getting out here and seeing it in the real world."

"Sarah's at Larchmont College," Dean told Steve. "That's how we met her."

Steve nodded with obvious recognition, which surprised her. Larchmont was well respected by those on the east coast, but it wasn't much heard of out here.

"Steve's knows the Charlotte area well," Dean said. "He retired from racing just a few years before me."

Sarah finally made the connection. If she hadn't been so distracted by whatever this strange current was that ran between them, she would have recognized his name immediately.

"Oh, of course," she said. "I've heard about your racing accomplishments, Steve."

He smiled. "And now I'm working to be known for my vineyard's accomplishments. So tell me…how do you feel about our NASCAR world so far?"

"Interesting…surprisingly complex…." She smiled as a parallel occurred to her, and then she raised her glass in salute. "Very much like your wine."

"And very much like you, too, I think," he replied.

Sarah didn't believe in all of that romantic nonsense,

like the crowds melting away until there were only two people left in the world, but this moment seemed to be coming darned close. She wasn't sure how long they stood there simply smiling at each other, but however long, she could have gone longer.

Dean cleared his throat, then nudged his friend. "Hey, we'd better get down to pit road if you want a chance to see your godson before the race."

"Right," Steve said absently, then repeated the word in a firmer voice. "Patsy, will you and Sarah be coming down to Kent's pit stall, or did you have other plans?"

Sarah glanced at Patsy. She'd told Sarah on the flight to Sonoma that watching her son race wasn't something she did particularly well.

"We don't have to," Sarah began to say, but Patsy cut her off by telling Steve and Dean that they would be down directly, and the men should go on ahead.

"Really, we don't have to do this," Sarah said. "If you'd prefer to be in a suite, I have some track management folks I need to chat with. We can just head on up and watch from there."

"Oh, no, it wasn't my little issue with watching," Patsy said. "I'm trying to get better about that for my daughter-in-law's sake. I just wanted to know without the men here to eavesdrop…what was *that* all about?" She tilted her head in the direction that Dean and Steve had taken.

"I have no idea," Sarah replied with absolute honesty. She'd been in love twice in her life, and neither of those men had ever looked at her with such focus and intent.

Of course, she didn't recall being so immediately transfixed by them, either.

"That was some chemistry you two had humming along," Patsy said.

"It was that obvious?"

Patsy laughed. "Beyond obvious."

A warm tingle danced its way once again to Sarah's fingertips.

Chemistry. It just might be addictive.

STEVE HAD ONE QUESTION for himself, and damned if he could answer it. Specifically, what was it about Sarah Stanton that had captured his attention?

She had to be a good fifteen years older than the women he dated. At fifty, he could—and did—date twentysomething-year-old lingerie models and actresses. He liked them for their general lack of desire for commitment and their uncomplicated natures. Steve had been married twice and would sooner gnaw off his right arm than marry again.

Sarah dressed more like a nun than a catalogue model, yet he could tell from the way she'd sampled her wine—in fact, even the way in which they'd earlier watched each other—that she was one innately sensual woman. The contrast intrigued him, even if she wasn't at all his type.

Except that when he should have been meeting and greeting and talking up his wine in the Smoothtone Music tent, he'd spent most of his time speculating on how buttoned-up and hair-tied-down Sarah had landed in the middle of that more glamorous crowd…and then speculating what she'd look like with her hair loose and one or two buttons—or more—undone on her white, short-sleeved blouse.

Steve laughed aloud at just how fully and instantaneously he'd become wrapped up in this woman. Clearly, everything about her had caught his attention. And she'd sure kept it once he'd had the opportunity to talk to her.

"Want to share the joke?" Dean asked him as they walked toward the pits.

"No."

"Good enough," Dean said.

And that was the great part of being a guy. Steve knew that single question would be the end of any interrogation from Dean. But the bottom line remained the same. There was something quirkily attractive about Sarah Stanton beyond her subtle good looks, and that was all Steve needed to know in order to determine his next move. He'd made a fortune in racing based on his immediate reaction, and he'd carried that awareness into the rest of his life. Instinct was good. Overthinking could really mess with a guy.

"We'd better move it along if we're going to catch Kent," he said to Dean, who nodded and picked up the pace.

By the time they'd made it to the No. 414 car's hauler area and pit stall, they barely had time to get with the team for the opening prayer and the National Anthem. Back when he'd been behind the wheel of a car, this

moment had been spec...
fully present in it, with ...
churning with race strateg...
at his godson, he apprecia...

While the cars were lin...
Steve and Dean moved close...
view. Kent had been having an...
had still managed a clear victo... ...e of
the regular over-the-wall pit cre... ...ut of com-
mission—at Dover a few weeks a.... Steve wished he'd
been there to witness the win, but PR for Pebble Valley,
plus seeking more financing and working with his winemaker on budget and buying issues, seemed to take up
more hours than a day had.

When it came right down to it, though, he didn't want
to be one of those owners who refused to get his hands
dirty, any more than Dean did with Cargill-Grosso
Racing. Both of them had controlled their destinies behind
the wheel of a car and had no intention of stopping now.

"Should be a good one," Dean said from beside him.
"Perry told me that Kent feels the car is dead on…good
and freed up and ready to rock."

"Then we'll look for a win," Steve replied.

Perry Noble, who was Kent's crew chief just as he'd
been Dean's before Dean had retired, was one of the
very best in the business. Steve had no doubt that the
No. 414 car was perfectly set up. And it needed to be,
since this was one of the more challenging tracks, and
one of only two opportunities that NASCAR drivers
had annually to run on a road course.

...ays loved this race, and not just because ...e in the middle of wine country—a spot that ...en a favorite of his long before he'd bought ...ble Valley, which sat only a handful of miles from here. He'd loved the challenge of the twists and turns and hills on the course. And he'd loved beating the ringers—those drivers who showed up only for this race because they thought they had road courses down cold. They might have, but like many, they had underestimated the challenge of driving a car built to compete in a NASCAR race.

The checkered flag dropped, and Steve grinned at the roar of the fans cheering simultaneously. That was something he'd never gotten to hear from the inside of his vehicle. He trained his attention on his godson. Kent had qualified fifteenth, but quickly got down to the business of improving his position. The race was on Lap 10 when Patsy and Sarah arrived.

Steve watched as Patsy gave Dean a quick but tender kiss and wondered how it felt to have that much history with one woman. The couple had been together since they'd been teens, and while Steve had bolted from his marriages in the bad times, these two had stuck it out. They were sticking out another rough spot now, as speculation swirled regarding the whereabouts of Kent's twin sister, who had been kidnapped as a newborn and presumed dead for years. Steve knew that Patsy had always quietly held out hope that Gina was alive, while Dean had accepted the worst and dealt with the pain. But now, with new information and leads being pursued,

Patsy's hopes had been raised even higher, and Dean dreaded seeing her hurt.

Steve accepted that perseverance in marriage had in some ways made Dean a better man than he was, and certainly a luckier one, too. But Steve also accepted his personal flaws. One of them seemed to be the lack of a romantic-commitment gene. All the same, he motioned Sarah over to watch the race with him. An afternoon of commitment he could handle. With pleasure, too.

"Any questions yet?" he asked her.

"None so far," she replied, her attention now firmly fixed on the action in front of them.

Steve didn't mind that, either. It meant that he could take a moment to pick apart what made her so interesting. First, she was clearly out of her element, but it didn't look to be rattling her at all. He wondered if he'd manage to look as comfortable in one of her lecture halls.

Beyond that, she didn't even seem to recognize that she had something really special going on. He hadn't been the only guy checking her out at the party. Granted, she wasn't exactly showing herself off in that outfit of a white blouse and nondescript khakis, but with her slender body and perfect curves, she was a standout nonetheless.

And now that they were out from beneath the cover of the tent, he could see that her hair wasn't just the plain brown he'd first thought. It had a touch of red to it that came to life even under today's cloudy sky.

She looked his way and caught him watching her...

again. She frowned, then swept a hand back over her head while asking, "What? Is there something in my hair?"

"No," he quickly said.

"Okay, then." She gave him one last quizzical look before turning her attention back to the race.

He wasn't ready to lose her attention. "Any questions yet?"

She smiled, and lights danced in her gray eyes. "No, none that have occurred to me in the past thirty seconds."

"Do you want me to tell you about the road course?" he asked.

"The NASCAR layout is one-hundredth of a mile short of a full two miles," she replied. "The venue is one of the busiest in motorsports, with events booked here almost every day of the year."

Okay, so she wasn't clueless, something, now that he pondered it, many of his dates tended to be.

"Someone has done her homework," he commented.

"What would you expect? I'm a professor," she said dryly.

It had been a long while since a woman had made him laugh…really laugh, from deep in the gut.

"Point taken," he said.

"Besides, I've been invited to meet with some of the track officials just after the race. I think it would be smart to show up informed. I want to expand our track operations internship opportunities, and this looks like the perfect place to start, don't you think?"

It seemed to Steve that this was the perfect place to start a great many things. When the action down on the track was over, he planned to snag Dean and make sure that he had at least one more day with Sarah Stanton. As far as he was concerned, this particular race to pleasure had just begun.

CHAPTER TWO

NIGHT HAD LONG AGO FALLEN, and Sarah's jet lag seemed to have pushed past exhaustion to become a sort of distracted giddiness. She lay in her hotel room, the television on for company in the background, and her laptop computer open and connecting her with the real world back home.

Today had been nothing short of surreal—far from unpleasant, but definitely surreal. While she'd never had a shortage of male attention, it had never before come from someone like Steve Clayton. Then again, the Steve Claytons of the world rarely wandered onto Larchmont College's tree-lined campus.

Sarah settled in and scrolled through the e-mail that had accumulated in her university account. The newest was from Martin, her long-standing ex-husband and dear friend, letting her know where their Thursday night dinner group would be gathering. She sent back a quick note confirming her presence.

Martin and she had met as young associate professors at Larchmont and married impulsively. Less than two years into the marriage, Martin had strayed with a grad student. Sarah didn't much like cheaters inside or outside the classroom, so she'd filed for divorce. It had taken a few rocky years—and a disastrous and even shorter-lived second marriage on her part—but Martin and she had managed to build a friendship that she valued more than she could begin to express, even to him.

Just then, her phone, which lay on the nightstand, rang out with the opening bars to "Hail Britannia," the ring tone she'd selected for her ever-so-British ex.

"Do you never sleep?" she said in greeting to him. It was past two in the morning back home.

"Vampire hours, my love," he replied. "Why sleep when the world's finally quiet and I can concentrate? So tell me, how was your tumble down the rabbit hole and into the world of NASCAR?"

Sarah smiled at the allusion. "Interesting." Her smile grew as she thought of Steve. "Very much so."

"Better you than me, all the same," Martin replied.

Sarah had to agree. Even though he'd been living in the U.S. most of his adult life, Martin remained innately British, not to mention forever bookish and just a smidge of a snob. She wasn't sure that he could appreciate the amazing pleasure of something as fast, fun and uncomplicated as an auto race.

"Don't judge it until you've tried it," Sarah cautioned.

"Fair enough," he replied. "Care to meet for a late supper tomorrow and tell me all about it?"

"Can't," she said. "Change of plans. We're visiting a friend of the Grossos for lunch before we return. With the time change, I doubt I'll even be into my office on

Monday. I'm not much of a world traveler and jet lag has already knocked my legs out from under me."

"Then I'll cross off Paris for our next honeymoon…. Though I do rather like that 'legs out from under you' part."

She laughed. "Funny. If you're lucky, I'll let you take me to Paris, Kentucky."

They often joked that if they were both unattached when they hit fifty, they would remarry. At the rate they were going, being single at fifty seemed a likelihood. Sarah had no desire, however, to be married again. She had found that the risks inherent in the ritual were far too great for the small rewards it offered. And business professor that she was, it was tough to argue in favor of a skewed risk/reward ratio.

But a baby of her own…that was something she was determined to make a reality. In fact, she had raised the topic of being the father with Martin, who had been cautiously receptive. She knew they had a lot more talking to do, though.

"Well," Martin said. "No supper tomorrow and no Paris honeymoon. What *do* you have to offer?"

She pondered the reams of correspondence and paperwork awaiting her in her office, but then considered how much a part of her life Martin was. Not many women could claim an ex-husband as a best friend. And under no circumstance could she see her far more weasel-like, cheating second ex in that role. In fact, she preferred not to think of him in any role at all.

"Lunch on Tuesday?" she offered Martin.

"Lunch on Tuesday it is," he said. "Get some sleep, love…and dream of Kentucky."

Sarah was smiling well after she'd hung up the phone. Martin made such a marvelous friend. Too bad he'd made such a heartbreaking husband. Still not ready to sleep, she flipped through the cable television channels until she came across coverage of today's race. While watching the cars race in tight formation was fun, it had been so much more thrilling in person.

Steve's commentary had made the race so much more understandable, too. Drivers' moves that had looked nothing short of crazy to her had made sense once he'd explained them. It all had to do with timing, reflexes and a split-second calculation of what would work and what would not. And the more he had talked, the more she had liked him. Steve Clayton might be a NASCAR great and one heck of a sexy man, but he was still funny and accessible. And when she'd talked, he'd really listened instead of paying attention to the countless other people and events competing for his attention. She'd found his direct gaze sexier than even his muscled build and killer smile.

Sarah could hardly wait for tomorrow's lunch. She knew that what they had happening between them wasn't real or lasting, but she could still live in the moment and have some fun. She glanced at her computer screen, currently showing its screensaver photos from the trip to Venice she'd taken with her mom the prior year. And then she began to wonder….

Tomorrow wasn't a date, yet she felt some need to

follow her standard ritual of Check Out the Guy. In this day and age, one couldn't be too careful. Before she'd become thoroughly Internet-savvy, she'd once had a date with a man who'd turned out to have a record as the local grower of illicit substances. Granted, Steve was a bit more of a public figure, and the Grossos thought the world of him, but ritual was ritual.

Sarah pulled up her favorite search engine and typed in Steve's name. Her eyes widened when the results appeared on the screen. Over seven hundred thousand hits! She imagined somewhere in that information she'd be able to find everything down to his age when the tooth fairy first visited. She was more interested in current events, though. Just to amuse herself—and for a little eye candy—she narrowed the search down to images of him.

"Wrong eye candy," she murmured once the photos appeared. Her computer's screen was rife with shots of Steve and an endless string of sleek, pretty females. He seemed to have his own Girl of the Week club.

"Those have to be fake," she said to one especially overbountiful female's photo. The girl would be getting breast-reduction surgery by the time she hit forty. Either that or she'd need an industrial strength bra.

There were some variations to what was apparently Steve's favored theme of wide-eyed youth. Hair and skin tones varied, but all were clearly under thirty and surgically enhanced. Sarah might have asked herself what he saw in them, but the answer was apparent. And while she was sure that some of them might be smart enough, no single one could have his—or her—life experience.

Sarah blanked out the screen, shut the laptop and put it to the far side of the king-sized bed. Her disappointment in Steve was sharp. Sharp enough that she recognized it as anger.

"Ridiculous," she said, knowing that the word applied as equally to her reaction as it did to his dating choices.

She punched her pillows a couple of times, ostensibly fluffing them for a good night's sleep, but actually to let out some of her frustration. Still unsettled, she turned off the television and the bedside lamp and curled up on her side. Sleep wouldn't be coming easily. She was in an unfamiliar place and being assailed by unfamiliar emotions. Two minutes later, she gave up and turned on the television again, forgetting that she'd had it on the auto racing channel. The film clip must have been footage from an old race because there, up on the screen, were Dean Gross and Steve in their uniforms, laughing.

"Figures," she said and switched off the television for the final time.

She'd just met the man and would likely only ever see him in the company of the Grossos. She shouldn't care what he did in his private life or whom he did it with…even if those girls were young enough to be his daughters. On the bright side—and not that it mattered—she supposed he wouldn't be the sort to cheat.

Steve Clayton would never be with any one woman long enough to cheat.

STEVE HAD TO ADMIT THAT for a man who'd consistently taken crazy risks in life, he'd landed well. As he stood in front of the main house at Pebble Valley watching Dean, Patsy and Sarah drive up the long gravel road that climbed the hillside from the main road through the front acreage, he tried to see the place as Sarah would, experiencing it for the first time.

There were more elaborate vineyards in the valley, with tasting rooms overbuilt to the point of looking like wine theme parks. Steve had ducked every offer to own one of those. When he'd bought this place, he'd done it for both the top-notch winemaking operation already in place and because the main house's understated, low-slung Spanish architecture appealed to him. It fit into the landscape instead of overpowering it. And, as he'd known from the first time he'd come to Sonoma Valley, he fit in here, too. The rock stars and actors could have neighboring Napa. This was home, the kind of place where he could climb on a forklift and do some hard work and not feel like he was all about show.

Dean pulled up in front of the house and turned off the car. Steve opened Patsy's door and said his hello as she joined him, and sent Dean a "Hey, pal" as his friend came around the front of the car. Then Steve went to offer Sarah a hand as she exited the rear of the car, but she gave him a brisk shake of her head.

"I'm more than capable," she said.

He smiled. "I didn't doubt that for a second, professor. I'm just an old-fashioned guy at heart."

"Say, like Hugh Hefner? That sort of old-fashioned?"

There was nothing like being compared to someone over eighty years old to make a man wonder just what he'd done to offend a woman. Especially *that* eighty-something-year-old.

He gave Sarah a closer look. Another pair of khakis, but this time she'd mixed it up with a pale pink short-sleeved blouse. That wasn't the only subtle change. Her gray eyes held a spark of challenge where yesterday he'd been pretty sure he'd seen an admiration that had mirrored his own for her. And while he wasn't the sort of man to back down, he also liked to know exactly what he was facing before engaging the opposition.

He gave her a broad smile in answer to her question. She could interpret it any way she chose. And then he moved on to the more receptive among his guests.

"I'm cooking for us," he told Dean and Patsy. "Rosita is home with her family," he added, referring to the housekeeper who, despite the fact she was a good ten years younger than he, had decided upon her hiring that she was also his mother…which amused the heck out of his seventy-three-year-old mom when she stayed at Pebble Valley.

"Is there anything I can help with?" Patsy asked.

"Nope. I'm doing grilled chicken and vegetable skewers, and even I can't screw that up. But I figured I'd show Sarah around before starting. You and Dean can make the loop again, too," he offered. They'd been his guests many times since he'd moved here.

Dean hitched a thumb toward the bocce court that sat between the main house and the tasting room, which was back down the hillside a stretch.

"Maybe a game instead?" he asked his wife.

"You're on," she said, then added to Sarah, "It's the one game I can consistently beat him in. He's got no finesse."

Dean laughed. "Nice try. You're not going to rattle me that way."

She looped her arm through his. "Oh, I have others...."

"So, back up here in, say, half an hour?" Steve asked.

"Works for us," Dean replied.

"Ready for a tour?" he asked Sarah.

"Okay," she replied.

"How about if we start with the public face?" he asked, ready to lead her down to the new tasting room.

"Oh, I think I've seen your public face."

That spark of he-didn't-know-what was back in her eyes. He knew it was none of his business and didn't really know her in any real way, but he had to ask. "Are you feeling okay? You seem...I don't know... edgy?"

The brief battle she waged with herself was obvious in the tension in her shoulders and the little line that appeared between her eyebrows.

"I'm sorry," she finally said. "I'm being a bit sharp. Not enough sleep last night or something, I guess."

"It's okay, but if you're not up for a tour, we could just go relax out on my patio."

"No, I want the tour. Really."

He smiled. "Good." He wanted her to see this place, and he cared more than he should that he'd gain her good opinion.

Steve started down the drive toward the tasting room, and she fell in stride next to him. As he looked over at her, he thought again how much he just flat-out instinctively liked this woman. There was no fuss, no worry over whether the wind curling off the mountains to the east was going to mess with her hair or the gravel of the drive might hurt her shoes.

As much as he liked being seen—and needed to be seen—with his chicklets, as his thirty-year-old daughter, Mattie, called them, sometimes they weren't as much fun as they appeared. But he understood the value of celebrity in America.

Back when, it had annoyed him that he had to live his private life under public scrutiny. Each marriage and divorce, each subsequent relationship…all had been fodder for the reporters. He'd hated every damn minute of it, but had been powerless to make it stop. Then he'd decided to go with the flow. He'd figured that since he had no interest in being serious with any woman, he might as well leverage this cult of celebrity for business advantage.

The women he took out, they understood. The benefits flowed both ways; they got press for being seen with him, too. If a starlet truly burned to be a clothing designer, she needed name recognition to launch that line. Steve was more than happy to put his face out there for her. After all, the same press exposure sold wine, too. It also made for one inexpensive advertising campaign.

It had been a good run, but he had to admit that his interest in this approach had waned. He wanted a real life, one he could own. And he wanted people around him who didn't give a damn that he was a public figure. Say, people like the woman next to him…

"What?" Sarah asked. "You're beginning to make me paranoid, looking at me like that."

"Like what?" he asked, just for the jollies of watching her color rise a little.

"As though I'm a specimen in a museum."

He shook his head. "No, actually I'm looking at you as though you're a real, living, breathing woman who just happens to be a pleasure to be around."

Her gaze met his, straight-on and direct.

"Well, thank you," she said. "I am nothing, if not real. No fuss, no muss, as my mom has always said about me."

They walked past the bocce court, and Patsy's laugh rang out at something Dean had said to her.

"That's what I like about Patsy," Sarah said. "She's definitely better at the fashion thing than I am, but she's still…well…real."

"She is. And one of the best women I've ever known. We've all been together since we were pretty much kids," Steve said. "And through the bad times and the good, back when we could barely afford a night out for a beer and a burger, to now, she's been the same…the center of Dean's world, even when he wasn't being smart enough to realize it."

"They seem happy," she said, and Steve couldn't miss the note of wistfulness in her voice.

"How about you?" he asked. "Ever married?"

"Twice," she said. "One ended sadly and the other was an unmitigated disaster. I'm not up for trying again."

"Really?" He hoped she hadn't caught the note of surprise in his voice.

She had, though. Her laugh was short but rich. "Yes, really. I've been single for a decade, and I have to say it's been the best decade of my life. Don't mess with success, you know?"

"Always a good theory."

They were nearing the tasting room he'd had built to replace the pole barn that had stood here before. While quality wines were his top priority, the same thing that kept the chicklets on his arm had led him to invest in this new structure: visibility.

The tasting room, with its white stucco walls and adobe roof, echoed the quiet style of his home. Down here, though, he'd spent about as much on the landscaping surrounding the building as he had the building itself. Picture-perfect gardens and terraces drew in people. And the wines that he and Kyle, his winemaker, were bringing to market kept them as fans.

"Wow," Sarah said as they walked past low ponds bordered with lavender that flanked each side of the walkway into the tasting room. "This is gorgeous. Amazing."

"Thanks," he said, trying to sound less stupidly pleased at her reaction than he felt. "We spent a good year working on the plans before we broke ground. It's not my usual style, but it takes a whole lot of folks in the state and local government to weigh in before soil can be moved around here."

"It looks as though it was worth the wait."

He swung open the broad cypress door to the tasting room and held it for her. At least this time, she didn't make a snarky comment about his attempt at chivalry.

"Hey, Steve," said Suzette, one of the four tasting room staff currently behind the bar. Though Mondays were usually one of their slower days, they had expected—and received—a surge in visitors because of yesterday's race.

Heads turned as he said hello back to Suz and the rest of the crew. He welcomed the visitors and told the crew to waive the nominal tasting fee they usually charged for their current guests. As usual, that was enough attention for people to turn back to the wine and away from him.

"Doesn't it get a little weird, everyone doing double takes when they see you?" Sarah asked in a low voice.

"You get numb to it," he said.

She nodded. "Kind of like when my students see me out at a restaurant or shopping. Because I'm unexpected and out of context, they stare."

"Yup, that's pretty much the thing. When I'm out someplace, people tend to think that that they should know me, but they're not always sure why."

He led Sarah to the sole open spot at the end of the long wooden bar that occupied the center of the room. Merchandise took up the outskirts of the room, except along the back wall, which was almost all windows, affording a view of the courtyard with its twin fountains and wooden tables sheltered from the sun by cypress-green-colored umbrellas.

"A red or a white tasting?" he asked Sarah.

"Red, I think," she replied.

He recalled that she'd been drinking Chardonnay the day before. "You're an all-around wine lover, I take it?"

"Since my teen years. My mom taught psychology at a small college in Bordeaux for three years. Wine with dinner was expected, even for someone my age. I learned a lot, including when to stop sampling."

"I'm impressed," he said.

She answered with a small shrug. "I was just tagging after Mom…which I guess is how I landed in academia, too."

"And your father?"

"He left when I was six," she said.

This didn't sound like a good first-wine-tasting chat, so he waved Suz over.

"Let's start with the Petit Verdot," he said.

After they each had their pours, he told Sarah a little about the wine. This was one of two that were made from grapes grown right here at the vineyard, which was one of the reasons he'd chosen it. The other was that it was a little rare and unusual…just like Sarah.

"Very nice," she said after sampling it. "I taste a little blackberry and maybe a little toasted oak. How does it sell?"

He swirled his in his glass. "Well enough here on the estate, but it's not the sort of wine I've tried to push in the larger market. A Cabernet gets name recognition. It's the sexy wine."

"And sexy matters?" she asked.

"For marketing, yes."

Her nod was brisk. "Makes sense. So where do you see this vineyard in five years?"

He grinned. "Are you interviewing me for a job?"

She winced. "Sorry, it's tough to turn off the professor part of my brain. While I teach mostly management, I think I'm a closet marketer."

He got the sense that she was curious about everything, and he liked that, since he was, too. "In five years I don't see us producing any more wine than we are now. We're a boutique producer and should remain that. But I want us to get to the point where I see our wines aggressively bid on at auction, like I do some of our competitors'. We have the quality, but we're not especially well known yet."

"And how did that happen?"

"The vineyard itself has been around since the 1980s. When a prior owner was ready to retire, he sold out to a beverage conglomerate that was buying up land in the valley. The conglomerate held on for ten really rotten years while it tried to make the wine industry function in a way that it never will, and then it put everything back on the market. That was good news for this place and others like it, who'd basically been stuck in neutral for those years."

"So what you made buy Pebble Valley?"

"My winemaker, whom I'd known casually for a lot of years, came to me and said he'd found a spot where we could make a name for ourselves. The original owner had bought the place back, but couldn't afford to keep it. My friend had the training, but not the money, and I had the money, but not the training." He looked out the far window to the terrace and the vista beyond. "But it was more than that.... Have you ever arrived someplace you'd never been before and felt like it was home?"

She absently ran one fingertip around the rim of her glass. "Yes."

"Well, that's why I own this place." He laughed. "Or at least why the banks and I own this place. I'm trying to get the banks out of the loop. It's too much work pressing the money out of them. I'd rather be pressing the grapes and growing the business with private capital."

She tilted her head as she looked at him. "You really *like* business, don't you?"

"Does that surprise you?"

"In a way, yes. After all the excitement of being a race car driver, this must seem quiet."

"There's excitement around here." He thought back to last year's harvest, which had stretched into early November—far later than anyone had been prepared to staff. "Sometimes too much. But I like the planning and the tactical end of the work better than the showy stuff."

"No way!"

"Yes, but if you tell my publicist I said that, I'll say you lied."

Laughing, she touched her empty glass to his. "Fair enough."

He glanced at the crew behind the bar, who he just realized were watching him. They were giving him broad smiles. It was nice that they liked seeing him look something other than tense with the details of making this place fly, but he could use a little more privacy all the same.

"Okay, the next wine I want you to try hasn't made it to the tasting room yet," he said to Sarah.

"Intriguing," she said. "Lead on."

Steve smiled. Lead on, he would.

CHAPTER THREE

HOME.

Steve had said it, and Sarah had felt it the moment she'd pulled off the wine trail and onto Pebble Valley's rolling terrain. She'd been to Bordeaux, toured Tuscany, and sipped Tempranillo in a Spanish *castillo*. Never, though, had she felt this sense of belonging. But this was Steve's place and never would be hers. Lucky man. Intriguing man, too.

Sarah was an expert at reconciling things…people… events. This was part of her job, teaching others how to perceive matters and make them mesh in the best way possible. But she couldn't reconcile the smart and driven man now leading her to the barrel room with the grinning guy in countless photos. The one who'd looked darned thrilled to have those girls draped over him. Something didn't add up. Either he was putting on a good show for her or one for the rest of the world. But one lunch wouldn't be enough for her to delve to the bottom of that particular issue. Better to enjoy the day and treat it as the wrap-up of her little vacation from the real world.

"I take it this part of the tour isn't for the public at large?" Sarah asked as they approached the large, metal-sided building that sat down a side drive, close to the main road.

"This is the private face of the business that I mentioned," he said. "Wine is as much chemistry as it is romance."

Funny, but she could see an overlap; despite her best efforts not to, she was feeling a little of both when it came to Steve Clayton.

He pushed the code on the building's security pad, and they entered. The room was cool and the light dim. Sarah drew in a breath as she took in the massive and shiny stainless steel tanks in their spotless surroundings. No, it wasn't romantic, but it was impressive. She stood in the middle of the large space while Steve went over to a set of shelves against one wall and pulled two glasses.

"This is a red blend we'll be bottling soon," he said on his way to a tank midway down the room. Sarah followed after him.

"Kyle, my winemaker, has a winner in this one," he said as he opened a tap just enough to send a small stream of the ruby-colored liquid into one glass, then handed it to her.

Sarah waited until he'd poured himself a short glass before holding hers up to the overhead light to catch its full color. Then she closed her eyes and narrowed her focus down to its rich, earthy scent.

Ahh... *This* was the romance of wine. This was where she could imagine a warm fireplace, the scent of pine garland rich in the air and a man—a very, very fine man—next to her.

"What are you seeing?" Steve asked. "Based on that smile, it has to be good."

She opened her eyes, and her smile grew. "Incredibly good."

She had no idea what made Steve look at her as though she were the hottest thing he'd ever seen, but who was she to turn her back on such a stroke of luck?

Sarah took a sip of the wine and savored it. As she swallowed, she tipped back her head and let the entire experience roll over her.

"It's a winner, all right," she said to Steve.

He said nothing in return, instead taking the glass from her hand and then setting it, along with his own, on the ground near the foot of the tank.

"I'm going to kiss you," he said.

He drew her close and watched her with an intensity that sent a hungry shiver through her. He hadn't asked her permission, but he was giving her time to object. Sarah might have had her reservations, but she didn't have an objection in the world. She wanted to know his taste much more than she'd ever wanted to know that of any wine.

He brushed the thick pad of his thumb in a line just below her cheekbone.

"Classic," he murmured as his mouth came teasingly close to hers, but then moved away.

Another tingle danced along her skin. Her hunger, an impatient creature, told her that he was teasing her, but her passion counseled that he was savoring the moment, and that she should, too. And so she let her hands settle on his broad shoulders and let her gaze meet his fully on, no hiding her curiosity or her anticipation.

His blue eyes shone with humor. "You're not in the least unsettled by me, are you?"

"Should I be?" she asked, though the answer was apparent in the high-speed drumming of her heart.

Instead of replying, he drew her close and kissed her with the same head-on passion she'd encountered from him thus far.

Should she be unsettled by him?

Oh, yes.

Sarah had been kissed countless times in her life, but this moment—this kiss—was different. Steve made her not want to think, and she *never* shut down her mind. But for this one crazy, forget-the-consequences moment, she would. As thoughts of propriety slipped away, she let herself just feel. When those twinges of conscience over kissing a relative stranger returned— and they would—she'd have an idyllic memory to balance against them.

Their mouths fit perfectly. No awkwardness, no fumbling. That was one of the cooler things about being a bona fide adult; she knew what she was doing and knew how she liked it done. The warmth of his body, beneath the fine cotton of his polo shirt, enveloped her. He wore some sort of cologne, nothing over-powering…just a spicy hint that made her want to nestle closer, so she did. And when he sought more from her, she gave willingly, hungrily. This was what *she* wanted. This kiss was for her.

STEVE KNEW FEW REGRETS IN LIFE, but choosing this place to kiss Sarah had just made the list. Yeah, he'd gotten them someplace relatively private, but not private enough for what he wanted to do.

He wanted to slip that prim pink blouse off her shoulders and see if her skin there was as ivory-white as he'd been speculating. He wanted to feel the curves of her body intimately. And he wanted to do it all day long. But since he could do none of that, he'd make this kiss count for one helluva lot.

Steve wasn't an unusually tall guy, just a shade under six feet. It seemed, though, that most of the women he'd held lately had been wearing stiletto pumps that made them nearly nose-to-nose with him. Well-grounded Sarah, in both shoes and attitude, seemed smaller in his arms. For whatever reason, that jazzed him even more.

He drew her tighter, and the soft sound of desire that she made sent him to the point of not caring who might walk in or how inconvenient it might be. He needed his hands against her skin. And he needed all of this right now.

In one of the greater strokes of luck he'd recently experienced, Sarah seemed to want the same thing. She had moved her hands to the back of his shirt and was tugging at it. While working to free the hem of her blouse from the waistband of her khakis, he edged the two of them back toward the wine tank. As he slowly danced them backward, his foot hit one of their wineglasses. The sharp sound of it toppling over jolted him.

What was he doing? He never lost control.

Okay, so he had the general gist of what he was doing. But even if they weren't interrupted—and they would be—was this smart? Did he really want this? Obviously, parts of him wanted this. Still his brain—an organ he'd come to really appreciate over the years—was waving a caution flag, and he needed to slow. Even if he didn't want to.

He gentled both his kiss and his grip on her, giving himself a chance to calm. After a moment he was able to accept that he'd probably survive moving away from her.

"I think we've got ourselves a case of poor timing," he said.

"Poor, but not impossible," she replied.

Her lips were full, her cheeks rosy, and he was pretty sure he was insane to be stepping back. But he needed to follow his instincts.

He feigned a glance at his watch. "We should probably catch up to Dean and Patsy. I've got to get lunch cooking, and…" He trailed off under the assessing look she was giving him.

"Right," she said. "Absolutely."

He'd just come up short in her eyes, and that stung more than it should have.

She bent down and picked up their wineglasses, then carried them over to the shelf he'd gotten them from. Steve just stood there, trying to figure out what the heck he'd been doing…not to mention what the heck he wanted to be doing.

"Are you coming?" she asked over her shoulder as she headed toward the door in long strides.

"Sure," he said.

Not often in his life had a woman led the way. He kind of liked the view, if not the feeling. There had been a time when he'd welcomed challenge in relationships…not exactly the sort of emotional and intellectual challenge that Sarah would pose, but a challenge nonetheless. Right now, though, his business was challenge enough. Why not leave his love life uncomplicated? That was, if he hadn't just complicated it already.

SARAH COULD FIND NO REDEEMING factor in being saved from herself. First, she'd do her own saving, thank you very much. She didn't need a man to do it. Second, she hadn't exactly wanted saving. She would have been somewhere beyond perfectly happy to have continued that kiss until her reason had returned. And she hadn't been in any hurry to have reason return, either.

Evidently, Steve had.

"It looks like Dean and Patsy are done playing," he commented as they passed the now empty bocce court.

She could have let the observation slip by, but she just didn't feel like it. "It must be a slow day for play."

He nodded hello to a couple of tourists who were passing them, apparently just coming back from a viewing of the public gardens.

"Do you think you can save the pointed commentary for a few minutes?" he asked her once they'd passed. "I know I've ticked you off and I'd like a chance to explain once we're alone."

She gave him a one-word assessment. "Unlikely."

"That I can explain or that we'll be alone?"

"Both."

She was angrier at herself than she was at him. He'd done nothing more than take what she had willingly offered...and then refused it. That was a risk inherent in any encounter. But offering it at all had been her choice, her risk. And her mistake. All actions had consequences, and this flirtation with letting reason slip away hadn't been worth the discomfort she now felt.

"Would you like a quick tour of the house?" Steve asked as they neared its shady front portico.

"No, thank you. I think it's better for both of us if we rejoin the Grossos."

"So you *do* plan to avoid me. That's very adult of you," he said.

She stopped dead in her tracks, then took a deep breath in order to push away the emotion still coursing through her.

"Actually, I am being an adult. I suspect that at this moment, whatever you say to me, I'll end up wanting to say something incredibly rash in response. I'm here as your guest, and of the many things my mother tried to teach me, 'don't argue with the host' really stuck."

Pity her mother had never added "don't make out

with the host in his barrel room" to that list of social graces. Then the upcoming lunch wouldn't be sounding like death by a thousand paper cuts to Sarah.

He shrugged. "If some rule of etiquette makes you feel better about your frosty attitude, that's great."

Steve led her past the front door and down a sidewalk edged with Mexican tile that wound to the back of the house. There, Dean and Patsy sat side by side on a bench at a long wooden dining table.

"Want to come grab a few things in the kitchen?" Steve asked Dean.

"Sure thing," he replied.

Steve walked off without so much as a backward glance at Sarah. She worked up a bright smile for Patsy, one that might have come off as more manic than cheery, based upon her friend's quizzical expression. It had been worth a shot, but Sarah had never been much of an actress.

As the guys headed off to the house, Patsy said, "Come sit."

Sarah might have been able to avoid Steve, but she would not—and should not—avoid Patsy.

"Did you enjoy your wine tour?" Patsy asked as Sarah took a seat opposite her at the table.

"Yes."

Patsy smiled. "I can see that."

Sarah instinctively tried to smooth her hair, which she knew was escaping from the knot she'd anchored it in while hurriedly getting dressed this morning.

"That's not the only tip-off," Patsy said.

Sarah glanced down at her blouse, but it had held up to the prior events.

"Your color. You look like a woman who has been kissed."

"Or maybe has done a little kissing," Sarah added.

"Really?"

"It was nothing. Just curiosity."

Patsy laughed. "No doubt. And now that it's satisfied?"

"It's finished," she said firmly. And she meant that, too.

"All right, then. I didn't think he was quite your type."

The sparkle in Patsy's eyes left Sarah wondering if she'd said that last bit more as a nudge at Sarah than as her real assessment.

Sarah looked through the broad set of double doors that Steve and Dean had entered when going into the house. Steve stood facing her way on the opposite side of an island in what looked to be one incredible kitchen. Dean's back was to her, but he must have said something funny, because his friend's face split with a broad grin. Steve must have felt her watching because his attention slid her way. Their gazes locked, and in that moment, she knew they were both thinking of one thing—that kiss. She could almost see him shake off the thought before he looked away.

Not her type? Steve Clayton was exactly her type…yet another man who would never quite fit into her life.

WHEN ASKED WHAT HE MISSED most about racing, Steve generally replied that it was a toss-up between tactics and winning. Of course, strong tactics increased the odds of winning. Already he could see that he had two problems regarding tactics and winning with Professor Not-So-Prim, out there on his patio.

First, in racing, the meaning of a win was pretty easy to grasp. Less so in life, and especially with this woman. There was something about her, and it was more than the way she'd turned him on…though there was no ignoring that, either. But without knowing what he wanted of her, he was going to be far from a tactical master of the situation. The very best he could do was hang on until he could figure her out.

"So, are you taking Sarah to New Hampshire next weekend?" he asked Dean while pulling out the cooking tools to grill the marinated chicken and vegetable skewers that Rosita had left in the refrigerator for him.

Dean looked over his shoulder, then back at Steve. "If she can keep Patsy smiling like she is right now, I'd take her anywhere."

While Patsy put on a good public persona, even Steve could tell that family matters were weighing on her.

"It's been tough, this whole Gina thing, hasn't it?" he asked, referring to the recent gossip about their missing daughter's fate.

Dean took a swig of his beer, then set the bottle back on the black granite counter before answering. "Tougher on Patsy than she's been letting on, even to me. But when she thinks I'm occupied with something else, I've seen her let down her guard. I've seen the stress and the sorrow. I'd do anything to make it go away, but I know we have to ride it out, like we have so many other things.

And in the meantime, there's nothing like a new friend to give her something else to focus on."

"It makes sense to me," Steve replied. And of course it furthered his personal campaign to see Sarah again without exactly having to state to her the extent of his interest. His gaze was drawn to her again. She was laughing at something that Patsy had said. She looked so relaxed and real that it seemed almost surreal to Steve. It was as though she'd made this place and this day her own without even trying.

Dean gave Steve a speculative look. "Why the curiosity about Sarah?"

"I like her." He shook his head. "Actually, I don't know if *like*'s exactly the word. She…interests me."

Dean laughed. "That's a new way of putting it."

"I'm not saying I don't think she's hot in her own professorlike way. I'm just saying that's not what I'm talking about, okay?" He knew he wasn't making much sense, but none of this made sense to him.

"Sure. But before you confuse me any more, let's just drop it, okay?"

Steve was cool with that. "Any problem if I tag along next weekend? I have some wine business in Charlotte on Saturday."

"No problem at all," Dean said.

Steve gestured outside. "Don't bother mentioning it to the professor. I don't want to make a big deal of it or anything."

"Right," Dean said. "That's the way to make me think nothing's going on with you two."

"Nothing is," Steve said.

"Then why don't you want her to know you'll be there?"

Steve took a long swallow of his beer as he tried to come up with a rational response. Of course, nothing other than an "I'm full of it, and there *is* something between us" would fly, so he kept silent.

"*Now* are you going to drop it?" Dean asked after giving Steve a broad grin.

Steve slid a pair of tongs across the counter to his friend.

"Drop what?" he asked with a deadpan expression. "I don't know what you're talking about."

"Better," Dean replied, then pointed the tongs at him. "Now see if you can work on that act before we're back outside with Patsy. One sign of interest in Sarah and my wife will have you two roped together so tightly that you'll never get away."

Funny thing. That didn't sound too bad to Steve.

CHAPTER FOUR

TUESDAY MORNING SHOULD HAVE been pretty standard fare for Sarah, but after having been away it was almost as though she was viewing Larchmont's campus through the eyes of a stranger. The college grounds, centered around a former abbey, were idyllic. This time of year, when students were few, they were remarkably peaceful, too. But Sarah was missing out on that peace factor.

The rest of her time at Pebble Valley had gone smoothly enough, if one discounted the speculative glances that had passed around the dining table with more frequency than the plate of chicken kebobs. Patsy had been the boldest at the game, but she'd looked so darned pleased at the idea something might be simmering between Sarah and Steve that Sarah hadn't been able to give her even a mild correction on the long plane ride home. Instead, she'd finally—blissfully—slept, certain that once she again walked on the rolling green hills of her campus, life would no longer seem so odd. Except that it did. She couldn't get Steve Clayton from her mind, and this was not good.

Just before eight, she entered Carlyle Hall. Bypassing the elevator, she took the stairs to the fourth floor, which held the bulk of the small college's faculty offices. Most were silent this time of year, but a few had their doors open. Among them was Martin's office.

He smiled when he saw her. As it had the first time he'd given her that crooked, self-deprecating smile almost fifteen years earlier, her heart warmed. There was something about tall, endearing, shaggy-haired Martin that just worked.

"It's about bloody time you're back," he said. "Did you miss me?"

She smiled. "As much as always."

He laughed. "Let's not take the time to analyze what that means."

Ah, how she loved the familiarity of this man. They had known each other so very long that their relationship had taken on a comfortable rhythm. Love, but not *in* love. Sarah didn't mind that one bit.

"Coffee break?" she asked.

Martin rose from his desk chair. "Thought you'd never ask."

They walked in companionable silence to the lounge at the far end of the hallway. The space, which also doubled as a small dining room, was empty. Sarah pulled the pot from the coffeemaker and frowned at the rather thick and suspect-looking contents. It appeared to have been simmering since yesterday. While she emptied the pot into the sink, Martin cleared the filter and set it up for a new pot of brew.

"So tell me about Sonoma," he said. "Was it educational?"

Yes, and then yes, again, in ways she had no intention of mentioning to Martin. Why, she wasn't sure. It wasn't as though Martin was especially proprietary about her on a romantic level. When he'd been dating Celine, a longtime girlfriend from whom he'd recently parted, they'd even double-dated on occasion. It had never seemed weird or forced, so she had no reason to be secretive about her encounter with Steve. All the same, she chose to keep that bit of her trip to herself.

"Sonoma was wonderful, especially the race," she said. "It was nothing like I had imagined. It was noisy, yes, but in the best of ways. The Grossos have invited me up to New Hampshire this weekend, and I can't wait."

She glanced over at Martin as she settled the coffeepot back on its burner. His expression was quizzical in the understated way only Martin's could be.

"I'm gushing, aren't I?" she asked.

"You are," he said, and then reached into the dishwasher for two clean mugs. "It's rare and rather entertaining, really."

She laughed. "I'm glad to be of some value."

He set the mugs on the counter, then came over to her and tipped her chin up so that their eyes met. "You, love, are of great value."

What he'd done to end their marriage was years in their past, but sometimes it seemed to Sarah that Martin still tried to make up for having cheated on her. It wasn't necessary, really. She'd learned her lesson in matters of the heart. While she could never control another human, she could control her choices. She deserved absolute faithfulness. Absent the man who could give that—one who was apparently rarer than a unicorn—she was content to stand alone.

"I know I am," she said to Martin. "I'm just glad that you caught on."

He brushed a fingertip against her cheek before stepping away. "I might be slow, but I do learn."

While the coffee finished brewing, he caught her up on office politics. Ted Carmichael, who'd been a thorn in her side when she'd been in the college of business, had gotten word yesterday that he'd received a prestigious grant. Bully for Ted, she supposed. This nudged him yet another step ahead of her on the tenure track. Sarah set aside any worry on that front.

Really, she sought flexibility more than she did the ultimate security of tenure. Flexibility would allow her to be a working mother, which was why she'd taken this new job. While she knew that her work was appreciated by the college's administration, she wanted to be seen as someone who would go the distance for Larchmont. Perhaps then they'd be more willing to go the distance for her, too. When she had her child, she wanted to slow down, but not stop. Economic necessity aside, work— and these people—were too much a part of her life to ever let go completely.

When the coffee was done, she poured mugs for herself and Martin.

"Where would you like lunch today?" Martin asked.

Sarah, who'd been just about to take a sip of her coffee, paused. "Lunch?"

"The meal after breakfast, also one you'd promised to share with me today?"

Now she remembered.

"It's up to you," she replied.

"Do you have plans to stay at the office all day?"

"Not really."

"Good, because then I know just the place to give a try for a late lunch…say, around two o'clock. There's a new bistro that opened last week in uptown Charlotte. Their wine list is supposed to be amazing."

Wine.

One simple word and memories of kissing Steve swirled through her mind, as complex and potent as the drink itself. She tried with little success to push them back.

"Sarah?"

"Yes?" She sounded a little "not there" even to her own ears.

"Lunch, then?"

"Lunch? Yes, of course."

"Are you feeling well?"

"I'm fine, really. Maybe a little jet-lagged yet, but that's all."

He scrutinized her for a moment, and Sarah did her best to look as though she hadn't just entirely reeled back in time to when she was in Steve's arms.

"Nothing odd happened in Sonoma?" Martin asked.

She put a little spice back in her voice. "Other than the fact that I was there at all, no."

He chuckled. "We'll see if we can bring you fully back over lunch, then."

"Good plan," Sarah said as they exited the lounge, mugs in hand. She needed to come back. This was real, while Steve and Sonoma were the dream, not the other way around.

ONE MAN, TWO LIVES. Sometimes that was the way it felt to Steve, and he liked this private existence a whole lot better than his public one. He'd risen before dawn, not because he had any specific tasks to accomplish at that hour, but just because he was home—a rare thing, lately. He had wanted to spend time on his land.

Now it was almost eleven, and he had a visitor arriving in a few minutes. As he made his way up the drive to his home, he wished that he were back walking the rows of vines with Kyle, discussing the technical aspect of winemaking in the same way he used to discuss the technical aspects of racing.

Steve looked down at his denim-clad legs and soiled work boots. Maybe this wasn't the slickest garb in which to meet a potential investor, but it was the most honest. Other than when hosting Pebble Valley functions on the NASCAR circuit, this was who he planned to be from here on out: Steve Clayton, vineyard owner and apprentice to his own winemaker. Better that Damon Tieri, his prime investor candidate, knew this up front.

Steve reached for the hammered bronze handle of his home's front door, but it swung inward at the very same moment. If this hadn't happened countless times, he might have been startled. As it was, he was used to Rosita anticipating his every move.

"You've got to stop doing that," he said to his house-keeper/personal assistant/conscience and drill sergeant.

"And you have to start answering that fancy cell phone of yours. Why have it if you're going to ignore it?" she asked as she closed the door behind him.

He absently patted his pocket, then remembered that he'd turned the ringer to silent when he'd been watching the sunrise.

"It's there for my convenience, not the other way around," he said.

"Mr. Damon Tieri is also here for your convenience, I think?"

Steve hitched a thumb back over his shoulder. "I didn't see a car."

"His driver dropped him off, then left."

"Driver?"

Rosita nodded. "Limo, too. He looks like the sort of man who belongs in one…or in the movies."

Steve grinned at the sparkle in her dark eyes. "Careful or I'll tell Paul that you've got a crush."

Rosita laughed. "My husband knows he's my one and only, but a little admiring from afar never hurt a woman."

And in his unattached state, a little admiring from close up never hurt a man. He wondered what Professor Sarah was doing right now, and just how surprised she'd be to see him on Sunday. But he needed to put aside thoughts of Sarah and get down to business.

"And where is the current object of your admiration?" he asked Rosita.

"I put him in the den. I didn't think you'd want him

wandering your office alone. Better that you don't have a reason to cross this one off your list as you have the three before him."

Finding an investor was never easy, and finding one with whom he could strike the right balance of power was proving to be one of his toughest challenges yet.

"Tell Mr. Tieri that I'll be there in just a moment."

"I will." She walked a few steps away and then turned back. "You'll like this man, I think. He feels right."

From anyone else that would have been an odd statement, but Rosita had an impressive second sense about people. If she weren't running his world, she'd do well running a small nation.

"Good," he said. There was no denying that he needed money to bring Pebble Valley to the next level, but unless it was one hundred percent right, he wouldn't do it at all.

FIVE MINUTES LATER, STEVE—minus a lot of field dust— entered his den.

Damon Tieri was seated in one of the two leather chairs that faced the fireplace and the flat screen television above it. He was deep in conversation with someone on his cell phone. As a courtesy, Steve waited in the doorway as the younger man wrapped up his call.

Tieri stood and pocketed the phone while extending his right hand to Steve, who came forward and shook it. Tieri was probably an inch or so taller than Steve and he carried himself with an authority that Steve liked. He could also see why Rosita had swooned just a little.

Steve had heard the movie star comparisons thrown his way, but they fit the darker Damon Tieri just as well.

"Thanks for coming to visit," Steve said. "Have a seat and let's talk for a while before looking around."

His guest settled in.

"I take it you're serious about this investment," Steve said once he'd sat in the chair by Tieri's.

"Yes, but even if I didn't think Pebble Valley was an ideal investment, I would have come. I've been following Kyle Markham's career for a decade at least."

Steve had to bite back a smile. While being fifty years of age never sat foremost in his mind, sometimes the years did play in to his perceptions. He'd peg Damon Tieri as being in his early thirties, which meant that he'd have had to have been into wine when most college guys were chugging beer and downing shots. But looking at Tieri's impeccable custom garb and knowing his wealthy background and Ivy League education, Steve would buy in to the statement.

"Kyle is undeniably the talent here," Steve said. "And I'm going to do what it takes to keep him, but you need to know that I've been working with him almost daily. When he came here, he knew that part of the deal was to train me in winemaking. The first release we crafted together will be out next year."

"Then you don't plan to be a hobbyist or just the face of the vineyard?"

"No," Steve said firmly. "It's like racing. If I can't be one hundred percent into the game, I don't want to do it."

"Which is why you retired?"

"I had achieved all I wanted to, and much as I hate to admit it, I wasn't as hungry as the kids coming up."

Tieri nodded. "It's good to know when it's time to get out. How do you envision your role here?"

"I know that to some degree I need to be the face of Pebble Valley, but I want to ease out of that."

"Really? I'd have expected that you've become accustomed to life in the spotlight. Most people I've met like that are hesitant to let it go."

"I won't lie, it has its benefits, but I'm ready to move on. I'd rather be involved in decisions on the winemaking end than selling the wine to the public. It's time to let someone else take that on."

"Fair enough," the younger man said.

"As you know from the information I've given you, I've had consultants come in and analyze what needs to be done and the capital infusion required to make it happen."

"Let's be clear on one point. I'm not looking to be simply a bankroll, Steve. If I invest, it will be in a very active way."

This was a step Steve might be willing to take. Damon Tieri had quickly made a name for himself in financial circles as a hedge fund manager, but what had made him legendary was leaving the market at its very peak and making a fortune for himself and his clients. He had both wealth and the thing that Steve valued even more—good gut instincts.

"So long as we have a framework in place, I'm not opposed to having an active investor."

Damon leaned back in his chair. "And how do you see that framework being structured?"

"The financial end will be decided up front, and I'll leave that to the attorneys and tax advisors, but the land and house stay in my name. When it comes to decisions about the vineyard property and the wines…when we agree, great. When we don't, my vote carries."

"And in exchange for the power I've just hypothetically ceded to you?"

"You control the marketing. I'll give you my two cents, but if you see a better plan, it's yours to run. And you get the greater share of the profits since I want the land."

Tieri smiled. "I'm not opposed to more money."

"I didn't think you would be. Why don't we take a walk around, then talk some more?"

The younger man rose. "Works for me."

Steve chuckled. "Just so long as you understand that if we close this deal, *I* won't be working for you."

"That statement cuts in two directions," Tieri replied.

Steve stood. "As most concepts do. But let's talk about power-sharing later, once you've seen if you like the way we make our wine."

SARAH HADN'T REALLY EXPECTED to find Pebble Valley wines on the bistro's extensive list, yet she still felt a pang of disappointment that they weren't represented. And then she quashed that pang as firmly as she could. Pebble Valley wines were none of her business.

She looked around the bistro. Its simple café decor was a good counterpoint to the ornate architecture of the historical site that held it. The place was still busy given the late luncheon hour, but Sarah wasn't surprised. The menu had been as much of a gem as the wine list. She smiled as some peace finally settled into her bones.

"Now, there's the Sarah who left a few short days ago," Martin said, then raised his wineglass in salute.

She touched her glass to his, then sipped the Côtes du Rhône she'd selected. It was a classic French wine, not a whisper of Pebble Valley to it, thank heaven.

"And now that you're wholly back, I'd like to talk about this baby proposition," he said.

So much for calm Sarah. She hadn't been prepared to discuss this and was actually quite surprised that Martin would raise it on his own. But he had, and since she was the one who'd brought forth the plan in the first place, she could hardly shut him down.

"And what have you been thinking?" she asked.

"Any number of things from how we'd accomplish the creation of this baby to whether you see us as Mum and Dad under one roof?"

Now she was doubly glad that she'd agreed to share a bottle of wine. A minor amount of anesthesia was going to be required to get her through this discussion painlessly.

"Artificial insemination," she replied in answer to the first part of his question.

"The tried-and-true method offers better odds of success," Martin said.

"I understand the odds," she said. "But there are parts of me…of my heart…that I don't think I could give to you again. Lovemaking is too intimate, too personal for what we share now."

If he was hurt by her answer, he didn't show it. "But think of what you'd be missing. It *was* good between us…really quite phenomenal, actually."

"It was also a million years ago," Sarah said.

"Trust me, my memory hasn't failed me on that one point, at least."

She laughed. "You're trouble to the very end, aren't you?"

"And optimistic to the very end, too. Now about the living arrangements you propose?"

"Certainly I'd expect you to be part of your child's life. You'd be the father, after all. But I'd want sole legal and custodial rights."

He sat silent for a moment, and she watched the emotions play across his face…annoyance, first, and then a little sorrow, maybe.

"Sarah, despite our past, I wouldn't leave a child like your father left you," he said gently.

This was something she preferred not to address. She'd worked through her father's dead-of-the-night departure years ago. Her amazing and sometimes scarily smart mother had been parent enough to cover both roles.

"It just makes better sense," she said. "It's cleaner and easier to deal with."

"Why not just go to a clinic? You're looking for biological material, not a co-parent."

"I'm looking for more than that. I promise I'd never cut you off from your child. But as for clinics, I don't like the risks," she replied. "I don't like the idea of not knowing who the father will be. Do you remember Terri Browning?"

He frowned, then his face cleared as recollection dawned. "Your college roommate…the one who became the youngest partner ever at her Wall Street firm?"

"That's the one. I didn't share this with you since the two of you never got on so well, but four years ago, Terri decided that it was time to become a mother. She checked all her references in the detailed way that only Terri can, picked a top clinic to do the procedure and became pregnant."

"Happy result so far," Martin said.

"Yes, well, not for long. Her daughter was born with a genetic defect that should have been caught through thorough screening of the donor, but it wasn't. She died before she was three months old. It was heartbreaking, Martin. I don't want to run that sort of risk."

His smile was as crooked as ever. "At least not while you have good old Martin available, eh?"

Sarah's heart lurched; she never wanted to hurt him. "Please don't think of it that way. You know how much I care for you."

He reached across the table and took her hand. "I know, love. It's just that the reality of what we have stings a bit."

She squeezed his hand before letting go. "I think what we have is miraculous, and I can't think of another person on earth who'd be a better father to a child."

"But you don't quite see me as your lover."

"Exactly."

"Ouch again," he said. "But you're honest to a bloody fault, I'll give you that."

"Let's just take some time and let our feelings settle in, okay? I'm anxious to do this, but not in a hasty fashion."

He nodded. "I understand. But for the sake of my ego, perhaps you might work on curbing the bluntness?"

She laughed. "I'll try, but I haven't gotten very far with that in the past forty-two years."

"One can always hope," Martin said dryly.

Yes, one could. And Sarah hoped to find a way to keep her best friend and have a baby, too.

No DOUBT ABOUT IT, Damon Tieri was a detail man. Yesterday, Steve and the younger man had ended up spending until past sunset examining winery operations. Kyle, the winemaker, had been about to begin a Brix value testing, to determine the current sugar levels in their Chardonnay grapes. Steve had explained to Damon that one hundred berries would be plucked and their juices blended, then tested. The results would give a measurement of how this particular block of vines was ripening.

That hadn't been enough for Tieri. Instead he'd rolled up his shirtsleeves and asked to be part of the process. He'd helped pick a berry from every third vine and then asked a thousand questions as Kyle had blended, then tested the resulting juice with the refractometer. Discussion had gone on from there, to how Steve and Kyle decided what to plant, and what was the optimum grape production per acre, by variety of grape. This was the stuff that intrigued Steve, so he'd hardly noticed when the day slipped into evening.

Finally, Tieri had called his limo, but asked to come back in the morning. Steve had been all for it. He liked the man, and respected him, too. Now it was well past noon, and the two of them were back in the den, talking yet more—wine business, mostly, but a little NASCAR and other stuff thrown in. There was no mincing of words or getting ticked off over opposing viewpoints, even though they had their share of them. When it came down to that most important basic—the ability to communicate—they had it covered.

"This will work," Damon said with the same certainty that Steve was feeling.

"Let's get the lawyers cooking," Steve said while pulling out his phone to call his attorney. In less than a handful of minutes, both he and Damon were off their phones, and lawyers from coast to coast were beginning to rack up billable hours as they put the deal on paper.

Steve looked over at his likely new partner. "I've got a feeling you'll be seeing a lot of this place."

"Undoubtedly," Damon agreed.

"I'll have Rosita set aside a guest room for you and give you a set of keys to the house."

"That sounds better than a hotel, if it won't cut into your life."

"Not possible. This place is big enough and we're both busy enough that we'll be lucky to catch each other coming and going."

"It's a deal, then," Damon said.

"Assuming the lawyers work as well together as we do, yeah. Now how about some time watching business in the tasting room? We never made it there yesterday."

Tieri stood, too. "I thought you'd never ask."

Steve knew it for sure; this was going to be the beginning of a damn fine business venture.

CHAPTER FIVE

WHETHER A SATURDAY OR SUNDAY, race day morning had always been another work day for Steve, and catching a plane had been part of that gig. He'd always been focused on the next step, though, not the voyage. This time was different. He'd been looking forward to the flight just as much as seeing the New Hampshire race, and that change of events could be explained in two words: Sarah Stanton.

He glanced over at Dean and Patsy, who sat side by side in the private airstrip's lounge as they waited for Sarah to arrive. Last night, he'd stayed at their house, and it had been like the old days all over again. The three of them had played poker for pretzel sticks and laughed as they recalled some of the wild stunts his daughter, Mattie, had pulled when she'd been a teenager.

"I'm sorry I'm a couple of minutes late," Sarah said as she rushed into the lounge. "My car—"

She stopped dead in her tracks. Obviously, he'd been spotted.

"Steve?"

He rose. "It's good to see you again, Sarah."

"Yes, well…you, too."

He'd had warmer greetings, but he hadn't expected open arms after springing himself on her.

"Let's get rolling," Dean said. "We've got a race to see."

As Dean and Patsy made their way to the door, Steve hesitated to let Sarah proceed in front of him. His courtesy earned him a glare. Or maybe it was just his presence.

"May I carry your bag for you?" he asked, gesturing at her professor-perfect briefcase.

"I can handle—"

"I know. You can handle it yourself."

"Correct," she said.

He held one hand out before himself, palm up.

"After you, then."

She hesitated just long enough that he wondered if she was about to ditch the trip. Instead, she gave him one more suspicious look.

"Really, after you," he said. He didn't want daggers spearing his back all the way onto the plane.

The Grossos' jet had four seats plus a divan that seated three. Patsy and Dean had chosen to sit on the divan, and Sarah took a window seat in the second of the two rows. If Steve were feeling particularly diplomatic, he would have chosen a seat in the front row. He wasn't, though. He wanted this deadlock knocked off center, one way or another.

Without even giving Sarah a chance to object, he settled in next to her. She politely declined coffee from the steward without once letting her gaze even brush

Steve, a neat trick he had to admit. He waited until they were aloft to try to engage her.

"Nice day for a race, isn't it?"

"That kiss meant nothing, you know that, right?" she whispered to him.

Not quite the response he'd expected, but he'd take it.

"Nothing?" he asked in a low voice.

"Nothing. We're both adults and we can just move on as though nothing happened."

Steve managed to stifle his laugh, but he couldn't lose the grin.

"What?" she demanded.

"Do you really think that?"

"Yes."

He chuckled. "Then, professor, you've got some learning to do."

WHAT WAS IT ABOUT STEVE CLAYTON? Why did he have such an unnatural ability to get under her skin? As long as she had *some learning to do*—and how that phrase rankled even hours later—Sarah figured she'd add those two questions to the list.

She had to remind herself that Steve hadn't been antagonistic. Quite the opposite, really. And to be brutally honest, earlier this morning she'd been snappish. She preferred to attribute that condition to lack of caffeine after her car had refused to start, than to the fact that just the sight of Steve Clayton had warmed her up in a most unsettling way.

He'd left her alone the rest of the flight, which had

given her time to rebuild her defenses. Once they'd arrived at the track, he'd limited his comments to information that Sarah actually found quite useful. He knew just how far to push her and when to retreat. He was good. *Very* good. And she was a sucker for it.

Just a few minutes ago, Dean and Patsy had gone down to the pit area to greet both Kent's and Roberto Castillo's teams, but Steve had persuaded Sarah to accompany him to a private suite for a prerace reception. She'd agreed mostly because she didn't want to always be under the Grossos' feet. Or so she'd told herself.

The reception they now attended was smaller than the Smoothtone Music event where she'd met Steve. This was a gathering of maybe thirty people in a small but elegantly equipped suite, complete with an antique rosewood bar and vintage furnishings. She was thankful that she'd dressed up a little this time, setting aside her khakis and blouse for a pair of pale blue raw silk slacks and an ivory silk shell, and letting her hair go free. This was the fanciest outfit she owned that was also suitable race day garb. Still, though, as she looked around the suite, she realized that she was lacking the glamour element that so many of these women carried off with ease. Sarah made a mental note to have Patsy sort through her jewelry with her. She had a ton of old pieces from her grandmother, but could never quite figure out how to pull them off without feeling like the jewelry was wearing her.

"I've brought you a peace offering," Steve said, holding out a slender champagne flute filled with pale orange liquid.

"A mimosa? I love them!"

"Then I've succeeded in my mission."

She took the glass. "I suppose you have. Actually, I should be the one seeking peace with you."

His smile was intimate, warming his blue eyes. He had a way of making her feel as though she was the only female on earth, which wasn't such an awful thing, so long as she reminded herself that none of this was real. It was just Steve doing what he did best.

"I was rude, but before you go thinking that I want to take it all back, I still meant what I said," she warned. "I just went about it wrong. We do need to move on."

"Now, that I agree with. I just happen to think that moving closer sounds like one hell of a lot more fun than moving apart."

"Fun," Sarah murmured before taking a sip of her drink. Fun hadn't been a part of the formula for her in some time. Everything had been about her goals and the sacrifices required in order to achieve them.

"Yes, fun," Steve said. "Try it, I think you'll like it."

She had to smile. The guy had a point, after all. The last time she'd had flat-out fun, she'd had to consciously shut down her mind. She was sure a therapist would have a field day with that aspect of her behavior. Even Sarah recognized it as dangerously weird and to be avoided. The time had come to relax a little…in a controlled sort of way, of course.

"I think this place agrees with you," Steve said. "You look great today."

"Thank you," she replied.

"What? No objection to the compliment?"

"None at all. Bring 'em on."

"I like you, Sarah Stanton," he said.

"Good. I like myself, too," she replied, which earned her another broad smile from Steve.

If this was what it felt like to embrace fun, she planned to hug it tight for the rest of the day.

"Come this way," Steve said, and Sarah willingly followed.

Steve introduced her to the hosts of the reception, executives from NASCAR's tire suppliers. She was impressed by both Steve's depth of knowledge and the ease with which he included her in the conversation. By the time she finished chatting, she had yet another internship possibility in her pocket. If she stuck by Steve's side, her school year would be made. Of course, being by his side only increased the siren call of her libido, but she was a big girl and could handle that.

Steve put his hand on her waist and leaned close. "Want to go down with Dean and Patsy to watch the race or would you prefer to stay here?"

She let herself enjoy the tingle that passed through her. After all, that fell within the category of fun.

"What would you prefer?" she asked.

"I'd prefer to have you to myself, or as close to that as we're going to get in the middle of all these fans."

And in the middle of all of those fans, she could hardly fling herself at him, could she?

"Then let's stay here," she said.

During the race, as he had at Sonoma, Steve explained whenever she had a question. While she doubted that she'd qualify as a NASCAR expert anytime soon, Sarah was catching on to the rhythm of the event, which made it all the more fun to watch.

Then the totally unexpected happened; Trey Sanford's engine died, leading to a crash. Sarah drew in a sharp breath as the accident unfolded. She also grabbed and held tight to Steve's hand without intending to.

"It's going to be fine," he assured her. "Every year more safety features are added to those cars. It might look scary from up here, but Trey is surrounded by a cage that protects him."

All the same, Sarah held her breath until, just as Steve had promised, Trey Sanford emerged from his vehicle with no help.

"I can't believe you liked doing that," she said to Steve once Trey's car had been moved from the track.

He tipped back his head and laughed. "Well, not *that,* but the rest of it was one hell of a ride. And for what it's worth, I survived worse crashes than what you just saw."

"Insane," she muttered.

He gave her a mock glare.

"I meant that in only the nicest way," she said. If she'd thought she could have gotten away with fluttering her eyelashes at him, she would have.

"Of course you did," he said, then squeezed her palm.

She looked down at their linked hands, surprised that she still held on to him. It felt so natural. She looked up at him, and he smiled.

There was no denying it. Not only was she attracted to a man who had unapologetically spent years as the poster boy for arrested development, but that attraction was also growing. Never again would she throw around the word *insane* with such ease.

THE HOUR WAS LATE AS THE Grossos' private jet headed back toward Mooresville and their home. Sarah was dozing, her head nestled against a pillow that she'd propped against the cool window. Dean had stretched out on the divan and was sound asleep. The white noise of the jet cutting through the night sky was sending Steve in that direction, too. He had a commercial flight back to San Francisco International so early in the morning that his head hurt to think about it.

Steve let his eyes slip shut, thinking that a little rest was better than none at all. Sleep was almost on him when a sharp poke in the arm brought him back to full wakefulness.

He looked across the aisle at Patsy.

"What?" he asked in a low voice. He wanted Sarah to get her rest.

Patsy gave him a bright smile—too bright, in fact. "Have a good day?" she stage-whispered.

"Yes, but I'm dog-tired, now." He hoped that would be hint enough, but somehow he doubted it. There was nothing under the sun—or moon—more single-minded than Patsy on a mission.

"Sarah's something, isn't she?" Patsy asked.

"Definitely something."

"I think she enjoys your company."

"The feeling is mutual," Steve said, knowing he was only adding to Patsy's determination, but saying anything less would have been an outright lie.

"You know what I'm thinking?"

"I'm almost afraid to find out."

"I'm thinking it would be good for you to spend a little more time around here. We had such fun playing cards last night, and—"

"And you want me to spend more time with Sarah," he finished for his friend.

"Is that such a crime? It's a pleasure to see you interested in someone other than one of those empty-headed, silicone-injected little girls."

"They weren't all so empty-headed," he said in their defense.

"Mattie's mother was the smartest of the lot, and we both know she's hardly what we'd call well-grounded. Now, Sarah, on the other hand…"

"Just tell me what you have in mind."

"Stay with us clear through Daytona, next Saturday. We're having our big Independence Day cookout on Wednesday before heading south. Mattie's even going to be there."

She was pulling out all the stops by adding Mattie into the mix. Steve hadn't been a bad father so much as he'd been an absentee father. Mattie had lived in his house and been raised by some amazing nannies, but he'd been on the NASCAR circuit. Mattie had grown up independent, and now she was a whirlwind who came into his life unannounced and left before he even knew what hit him. He wished they had more than that, but she was grown and there was no taking back the past.

"I have to get back to Sonoma tomorrow, but I guess there's nothing stopping me from heading back this way. I was going to be in Daytona, in any case."

"So when shall we expect you?"

He smiled at Patsy's insistence. "Wednesday."

"Tuesday," she countered.

He winced. "I'm never going to get a night's sleep."

"Nonsense. I've seen you sleep in the corner of a garage through all sorts of racket. Sleep across the country."

He looked at Sarah, with her surprisingly long eye-lashes fanned against her lower lids as she slept. She was full of those little surprises, and he had certainly enjoyed discovering them so far.

"Fine, then. Tuesday," he said to Patsy.

"Good. You can take your nap now."

Steve chuckled. "Nice of you to let me."

"Isn't it, though?" She reclined her seat and closed her eyes, but a satisfied smile kept playing about her mouth.

Steve was feeling pretty darned good, himself.

STILL GROGGY FROM HER NAP during their short flight, Sarah walked to her car with Steve beside her. The late night air was laden with humid warmth when she could have used a good, cold breeze to jolt her to full awareness.

"Are you going to be awake enough to drive?" Steve asked. Under the glare of the parking lot light directly overhead, he looked as tired as she felt.

"Probably," she replied while fishing her keys from her bag.

"I don't like those odds," he said.

"No, really, I'll be fine." She pressed the unlock button on her key fob, and her car cooperatively came to life. She'd had her doubts after its sluggish start this morning. Sarah was about to open her car door when Steve settled his hand on her arm.

"Could you hang on a second?" he asked.

"Sure." She tucked her keys into her pocket.

He stood silent for a moment, and it seemed to Sarah as though he was marshaling his thoughts…and leaving her dangling.

"I don't know where it's going, this…this…attraction we have to each other," he finally said. "But I do know that I want more time with you. I want to see your home and meet your friends and just hang out with you."

Now she was fully awake. "That's a pretty bold statement from a man who lives on the other side of the continent."

He gave her a brief smile. "What are a few flights between friends?"

"Seriously, Steve…"

"I *am* serious. How are we going to know what we've got going unless we take the next step? I have to leave for the day tomorrow, but I'm going to take the red-eye and be back here by Tuesday morning. Can you find some time for me?"

"To…?"

"Show me what's important to you. Your favorite

park. Where you work." He shrugged. "Whatever suits you."

If she let him into her life instead of visiting his, how could she keep up her dividing line between fantasy and real?

"I can tell you without all of this cross-county hopping that when it comes right down to lifestyles, *we* don't suit," she said.

"Prove it. You're not backing down from a challenge, are you, Sarah?"

He knew just how to get to her. "Steve, this is crazy."

He brushed a kiss against her lips. "What about us hasn't been?"

He had her there.

"Give it a try. Give *us* a try," he urged. "It will be fun."

Fun right up until she could no longer protect her heart. But if Steve really wanted a trial run in her life, she would give it to him. It just might be the strangest ride he ever had.

CHAPTER SIX

STEVE SHOULD HAVE HELD OUT for a Wednesday arrival.

"My mother can be a little intimidating," Sarah was saying to him as she zipped down a country road at a speed that anyone other than a former NASCAR driver might define as a little fast. He didn't rattle easily, though.

Still, if he'd held out for Wednesday, the most perilous thing he'd have experienced was the potential of overeating at the Grossos' Independence Day bash. But, no. He wasn't even officially dating Sarah and yet here he was about to have lunch with her mother.

"Think a cross between Katharine Hepburn and a pit bull," Sarah chirped.

Okay, maybe she didn't chirp, but Steve was jet-lagged and sleep deprived, so he figured he was entitled to be a little jaundiced about the professor's utter cheeriness. That same cheeriness also smacked of a setup. Just over forty-eight hours ago she'd been hesitant at best to let this day move forward, and now she was acting like a cruise director on the Good Ship Lollypop. Something was up.

Sarah slowed, then turned left onto a broad, white gravel drive, at the end of which sat a long and low house with whitewashed walls and a steeply pitched slate roof that made Steve think more of France than rural North Carolina.

"Welcome to my mom's dream retirement cottage," Sarah said as she pulled up in front of the home and parked the car. "It would be in Provence, except I don't think Mom's quite ready to observe her favorite subject—*me*—from that far away."

"Subject? That's a little distant for a mom and daughter."

"I'm kidding…mostly. Mom was a psychology professor. She might be retired now, but she just can't help peeling back the layers on people. Me, especially."

He winced. "Sounds painful."

"Let's just say that it made for an interesting adolescence. Lots of empathy, but just as much bluntness. These days I accept that she can't really help the way her mind runs. Ready?" she asked, pulling the keys from the ignition.

Steve figured that "no freaking way" wouldn't be a palatable answer, so he gave her a pretty untruthful "sure" and exited the car.

As they headed to the house, Sarah paused to reach down and rub her fingers against the tall, silvery gray plants that lined the walkway.

"Lavender," she said. "I even love the feel of it."

And he'd love to be feeling something other than doomed.

The home's front door swung open, and Sarah's mother stepped out to greet them. She stood maybe an inch shorter than Sarah and wore her silver hair twisted into some sort of fancy knot on the back of her head. And thanks to his years spent dating the chicklets, he knew that Margaret's nubby-looking pale blue suit was vintage Chanel. She'd probably bought it while in her thirties.

"Darling," she said, then kissed her daughter on both cheeks. He tried to imagine his mom, who was more the suffocating-hug type, doing the same thing. The image simply didn't compute.

"Steve, this is my mother, Margaret Stanton. Mom, this is Steve Clayton. He used to be a race car driver."

Sarah could have given him a few more initial props, Steve thought as he extended his hand to the petite and elegant older woman.

"Hello, Steve," she said. To her daughter, she added, "And I believe Steve is now the owner of Pebble Valley vineyard, correct?"

"I am," he replied. He had immediately grasped Sarah's allusion to Katharine Hepburn. The pit bull portion wasn't as readily apparent. "Thank you for having me here."

"How could I not when you're the first man she's made an effort to have me meet since Martin?" Margaret replied as she ushered them in.

"Martin?" he asked.

"My first ex-husband," Sarah quickly supplied. "You'll be meeting him later, when we get together with the group from school."

There was no doubt about it; Sarah had set him up to run the gauntlet. Beyond not coming in until tomorrow, he should have been more specific about the things he most wanted to get to know. Say, like, if she had countless pillows on her bed or was more of a minimalist sleeper…

"Martin's a dear boy," her mother said, closing the front door behind them. "Though I think that when one has reached middle age, it's not quite the thing to still be so—" she raised one slender shoulder dismissively "—boyish."

"I don't know, Mom. That seems to be common among the men of my generation."

Steve was a little bugged at the way Sarah had thrown a challenging smile his way after saying that. From the outside, his life might look as though he hadn't grown up, but that was far from the truth. And he would never apologize for having had the guts and perseverance to grab his dreams.

He looked over at Sarah's mother. A fleeting half smile had tugged at one corner of her mouth. It seemed that like her daughter, she took in more than she gave out about herself.

"I could give you the sociological argument, I suppose, of how my postwar generation gave their children too much," she said. "Or I could just narrow it down to your particular truth of choosing the wrong men."

Ouch. Maybe a pit bull in velvet gloves. He was a little surprised by Margaret's bluntness in front of him, but Sarah looked unruffled.

"Those choices were made a very long time ago, Mom. I'd like to think that I've learned."

"Or at least avoided redoing," her mother replied while giving Steve the once-over.

He did feel kind of like a subject in an experiment.

"Shall we dine?" Margaret Stanton asked, then without waiting for a response, led them back to a sunroom off the back of the house.

Steve could tell this was a room that Margaret treasured. And as she pointed out a number of pieces that she'd collected in her travels with Sarah, he could also tell that she treasured her daughter.

Lunch was what Steve generally termed "girl food"—a salad with grilled vegetables on top and a loaf of crusty French bread cut sliver-thin. Good news was that Margaret had somehow gotten her hands on a bottle of his Chardonnay to be served with the meal. After half a glass, he was able to more amicably handle the fact that the vegetables weren't the only things to be grilled at Margaret's table.

"So, Steve, do you have any children?"

"Yes, one. My daughter, Mattie, is thirty, now."

"And no younger children?"

"None," he said. "Just Mattie, and she's enough."

"That, I can appreciate," Margaret said. "In her own way, Sarah was quite a handful. Stubborn as the day was long."

He laughed. "So I've noticed."

"That, she inherited from me," Sarah's mother said. She took a sip of her wine, then contemplated him for a moment. "So other than driving cars, what did you do for all those years?"

Sarah gave a choked laugh. *"Mother!"*

"Racing looks like a couple of hours, a few dozen or so times a year, going around a track, but it's a lot more," Steve said. "What I do now, at Pebble Valley, carries more personal risk, but I don't have the same sense of so many others depending on me to get it dead-right every time. Not only did I have my daughter and a couple of ex-wives depending on me, but also the team who supported me, and their families by extension, not to mention the folks at the companies whose products I endorsed. Now I'm a winemaker, but before I was a cottage industry."

Margaret smiled, and Steve could see where Sarah had gotten her knockout smile from.

"Point taken," she said. "At this stage of your life, it must be a blessing to slow down. Your retirement suits you, I take it?"

He laughed at her not-so-subtle needling. "Enough that I doubt I'll ever really retire. I need to keep busy, to keep learning."

"Are you college educated?"

"Not by a long shot. I think the teachers at my high school had a party the night I graduated. I was better at raising hell than raising my grades, and all I ever wanted to be was a race car driver."

"You're one of the lucky few who made it to a financially rewarding place without higher education. Surely you don't approve of that path for everyone?"

Clearly he'd struck a nerve. The only way he was going to get through this meal quickly and cleanly was to take control of the questioning.

"I don't usually go around approving of others' paths. I would hope, though, that people follow their passions," he said. "Do I think a college education is important? Yes. Could I have had one? Not easily, between my grades and lack of money in those days. Did I encourage my daughter to go to college and help her in every way I could? Yes, and she's an investigative journalist now."

"Very nice," Margaret said.

"Given the current conversation, I thought you might think so."

He could see that she wanted to smile, but barely masked it.

"Sarah was a straight A student," she said once the smile was completely vanquished. "Do you think you can keep up with that?"

And Ms. Straight A was now turning a spicy shade of red.

Steve grinned, both at Margaret's question and because Sarah was as much a victim of her own plot as he.

"Confidence in my abilities has never been an issue," he replied. "But I like to keep the catching up and getting ahead to business, now that I'm off the track. I think that in the rest of life…in relationships…people's strengths should complement each other and we shouldn't worry so much about who's in the lead."

Margaret nodded approvingly. "You might well have chosen an adult this time, Sarah."

"Mom, there was no *choosing*. Steve and I are just friends," she said, the red on her face not yet subsiding. "New friends. Very new friends."

"Whatever you say, dear," her mother replied.

Sarah looked to Steve. "Think you might help me out here?"

Steve leaned back in his chair and smiled. "What, and miss all the fun?"

This time, Margaret's smile was unstoppable. She raised her wineglass. "Here's to friendship," she said. "May a very new one evolve into a *very* good one."

Steve would drink to that.

SARAH WAS IMPRESSED, NOT THAT she planned to admit it to Steve. He had bearded the lioness in her den, and made her seem more like an elegant house cat. She thought back to her youth and the parade of boyfriends and near-boyfriends that had either fled or found a way never to face Professor Margaret Stanton again. Even Martin had said that he'd rather time-travel and face the Spanish Inquisition than have a meal with Margaret.

"Your mom's an interesting lady," he said as she drove them to a café on the outskirts of Larchmont's campus.

"Interesting is one way to put it," she said. "I've heard stronger adjectives used, too."

"For Margaret? Nah. She's a peach."

Sarah laughed. "Now you're pushing it."

"In more ways than one. If it weren't for your mother hinting that I'm nearing my dotage, I'd be napping now."

His weariness gave his voice a whiskey-tinged roughness that Sarah had to admit was rather sexy…not that she'd share that with him, either.

"You didn't sleep on the red-eye?" she asked.

"Worked," he said. "I actually do that…work, you know."

Apparently her mother had gotten under his skin a bit more than he was letting on, or maybe even aware. That was the thing with Mom. She had a way of getting a person thinking, whether one chose to or not.

Take Martin. Sarah had never thought of him as boyish, except maybe for his youthful appearance. But now that her mother had planted the thought, Sarah couldn't help but consider how little he'd actually changed in the years since she'd been married to him. Granted, that wasn't necessarily a bad thing. Or was it? He lived in the same condo, wore the same suit jacket and still fancied himself in his thirties…

Maybe boyish wasn't necessarily so good.

"You okay over there?" Steve asked.

"Me? Absolutely. Why?"

"You were frowning. Actually, it was more of a scowl, I think."

"That sounds attractive."

"I'm just damn pleased that you can."

"What?"

"Move your forehead. You know…BOTOX," he said.

"Never going to happen," she said. She'd earned her wrinkles, few though they still were, and she had no intention of paralyzing them into submission.

"Good."

She would have asked him what the heck the playmate set he most usually dated was doing getting all obsessed over wrinkles, but the whole topic annoyed her. She did wonder, though, what her mom would make of his dating patterns. That conversation would be well worth the pain of being picked apart herself.

They pulled up in front of the Good Earth Café. This time Steve winced as he took in the place's unapologetic 1980s not-quite-hippie exterior with its fishbowl-shaped windows and excess of stucco padding every surface.

"Let me guess," he said. "Hard chairs, vegan menu and wheatgrass shooters."

He was dead-on.

"Sorry, it was my friend Maya's week to pick the location," Sarah said. "I think this place brings her back to her undergrad days."

He gave a rueful shake of his head. "That being the case, I'm happier than ever that I went straight to the track."

"Come on, we'll make this stop brief, I promise."

And not just for his sake. Though it had seemed a good idea at the time, she really wasn't too hot on having Steve meet Martin. While Martin had strung together all the right words when she'd talked to him yesterday about bringing Steve to this gathering, something in his tone had seemed frosty.

"Ready?" she asked Steve before the impulse to pull out of the parking spot and just keep driving became too strong.

"For everything but a wheatgrass shooter," he said.

Which sounded fair to Sarah.

Inside the café sat the usual suspects at three tables pulled together along the back wall: ex-husband Martin,

Robert and Alden, who were in the motorsports program with her, Maya, who taught women's studies, Celine, Martin's ex-girlfriend, who was in the French department, and Howell, who taught philosophy. Sarah would lay odds that only Robert and Alden would have any idea who Steve was. She'd intentionally kept the details down to a minimum with Martin, describing Steve only as a friend of the Grossos.

They approached unnoticed by anyone but Martin. It was an odd moment, watching him take in Steve's rugged good looks. She wouldn't call the expression crossing Martin's features born of envy, but it was probably a close cousin.

"Hi, all," she said when they'd reached the tables. "I'd like you to meet Steve, a new friend from out of town." She then ran a quick verbal inventory of every one at the table, promising Steve there would be no quiz later.

Two open chairs waited at Martin's end of the table. Steve pulled out the one at the very end for her. This time she didn't object to the gesture, mostly to witness fiercely independent Maya's surprise. Once Sarah was seated, Steve settled in opposite Martin.

"So, Steve, do you also teach?" asked Celine, who was seated to his right.

"No, I own and run a very small vineyard in California."

"A vineyard? How elegant," she said, leaning nearer. "Napa?"

"Close... Sonoma," he replied. "And, believe me, all

the elegance is in the wines. The work itself is ninety percent hot and gritty."

Celine's thinly shaped brows arched and her mouth shaped into a little *O*, not unlike the café's windows. For a second there, Sarah wondered if the table was about to witness a reenactment of Meg Ryan's "When Harry Met Sally" restaurant scene.

"How wonderful," the Frenchwoman said.

Sarah had never heard Celine purr…until now. She certainly understood Steve's impact, even if she didn't especially appreciate witnessing it. She glanced at Martin, who was looking slightly queasy. She wondered if he still had romantic feelings for his ex. He'd told her that he had been the one to end it with Celine, but perhaps he'd just been saving face.

"Sarah can tell you all about the vineyard," Steve said. "She had a private tour when she came out to visit."

Sarah hid a smile at Steve's polite yet firm way of giving Celine the lay of the land.

"Then our Sarah was very lucky," said the French professor, looping a lock of her long black hair behind her ear. "And the wine, Sarah, would you recommend it?" she added after a slight pause.

"In a heartbeat," Sarah replied. And then her own heart began to drum faster as she recalled the intensity of that first kiss she and Steve had shared in the barrel room. A knee nudged hers under the table, and she met Steve's knowing glance. The smile they shared was intimate. It made her wish for other intimacies with him.

"Then this wine must be as intriguing as the vineyard

owner," Celine said. "Perhaps, if you come to visit again, Steve, you can bring some and we can have a tasting."

"I'd be happy to," Steve said. "I'm in the Charlotte area fairly frequently visiting friends I worked with before I moved on to wine."

Alden, who'd been watching the exchange between Steve and Celine, said, "Ah! Then you *are* Steve Clayton, the NASCAR driver, right?"

"Retired driver," Steve said.

"I thought it was you, but then it seemed almost ludicrous to think that you'd show up at the Good Earth with Sarah." A look of alarm passed across his ruddy face. "Wait… That didn't come out the way I'd intended. No insult at all meant to you, Sarah," he said in a rush.

"And none taken," Sarah replied. She had to agree that the whole scenario was out of the norm.

"I followed your career for years," Alden said to Steve. "I hated to see you hang it up. I'm betting you could have been competitive for another five years, at least."

"Competitive, yes. A consistent winner, no," Steve replied. "It had stopped mattering so much to me. I wanted other things and knew it was time to get out. But tell me about your work in the motorsports program, Alden. What's your specialty?"

And so the talk drifted from wine to academics to the near-whining that took place whenever college politics were discussed. Sarah was surprised to see that Steve managed to stay engaged in a conversation that even she found narrow. He asked questions about how the college departments were structured and what one had to do to get tenure, and he looked genuinely interested in the answers. In fact, the only member of the group who remained oddly silent was Martin.

Sarah excused herself from the table to use the restroom. When she was through checking her minimal makeup, he was outside the door waiting for her to return.

"I thought only females traveled to the restroom in packs," she teased.

He didn't even crack a smile.

"Is that man for real?" he asked.

"I take it you're referring to Steve?"

"Of course."

"And you collared me outside the bathroom, why?"

"To see if perhaps you had left your common sense in New Hampshire this time."

She held out her arms and turned a circle. "It's still me. Still the same old Sarah, overabundance of common sense and all."

"Ah, but Sarah doesn't customarily dance a pirouette…or hang out with mannequins."

"Come on, Martin. Cut Steve a break. Yes, he's not the sort of guy who usually drops into my life, but trust me, he's a warm, real, breathing man."

She couldn't quite help the smile that started from somewhere deep inside as she considered just how warm he was. Martin, however, was looking far from persuadable.

"He looks the sort to get his nails manicured, and not the kind of man I ever imagined you'd look at twice," he said.

"Actually, he's the kind of man most women look at twice," Sarah replied, not even bothering to dignify the "nails manicured" comment.

"My point, exactly. He's handsome to the point of being a walking cliché."

"Hey, being physically attractive isn't a crime. Steve's a fun, interesting man. You, for whatever reason, are determined not to like him."

"I neither like nor dislike him," Martin said in a chilly voice.

She wanted to laugh at his outright lie, but that would have been as hurtful as she was finding his current attitude. But she knew Martin, and understood how unbendable he tended to stand in the face of change. This had to be strange for him, witnessing her with a new man, and on the heels of that sight, Celine in full flirt mode, too.

"Please don't blow this out of proportion," she said. "Steve is a novelty to Celine. Of course she's going to be interested, especially if you're so obvious about it raising your ire."

"Celine isn't my concern."

"Then what's the issue?"

"You. You're in over your head."

Her breath left her body as she took the verbal blow. Was this how he saw her, as completely unsophisticated and incapable?

"That is quite possibly the most insulting thing you've ever said to me," she replied.

"I'm just looking out for your best interests."

"You are? I guess that's kind in a grossly misled sort of way, but I'm entirely capable of looking after myself."

He shook his head. "I don't know what's happening to you, but I don't like the change, Sarah, not at all."

But Sarah liked the change very much. For the first time in ages she felt a wonderful excitement humming inside her. Life had so many possibilities. All she had to do was set aside her aversion to risk and take what was right in front of her.

Or back at the table...

CHAPTER SEVEN

SARAH'S EDGE OF UNHOLY GLEE seemed to have worn off. Beneath it rested something that Steve couldn't quite identify. She seemed more focused, somehow, yet less intense…which made little sense to him, since focus and intensity always went together in his life. But why should he expect anything to make sense today?

They had sat with the professor pack for only another half hour when Sarah had glanced at her watch and exclaimed that the two of them were going to be late for another engagement. He'd had no clue what was to happen next, but he'd been glad to leave Martin and his obvious jealousy. Whatever the stuffy professor had done to lose Sarah was ancient history, and Steve figured that Martin should just get over it and move on.

"So who's next in the gauntlet?" Steve asked as they pulled from their spot in front of the Good Earth.

"No one," she said. "I just thought that even you must get tired of talking it up."

"You're right. And so now?"

"Maybe it's time for you to see more than the driveway at my house?"

He'd left his rental car there earlier today. It had been a nice driveway and all, but again she was right. He'd seen her reflected in the mirror of her friends, but he wanted to see her alone.

"Sounds good," he said.

Sarah was silent, and he was fine with that, too. He'd kept it up to full throttle while meeting her mom and friends, and the effort had come with a price. Steve was tired, the kind of weariness that only a full night of sleep would fix. But he was going to stay with Dean and Patsy tonight, which meant that once again, talk would take the place of sleep.

They pulled in next to his rental car, and Steve took a better look around than he had earlier. Then he'd been fixed on seeing Sarah. Evidently she'd been fixed on getting him out of there because she'd been waiting for him on her front porch.

Sarah's home was part of an older neighborhood where the houses sat close together, very unlike his spread in Sonoma. Still, he liked the warm feeling that the street gave him. The residences were a jumble of older architectural style, but all of them were attractive, though sometimes in a quirky "an artist lives here" way.

Sarah's house looked to be much like Sarah…small and elegant with a charm that sort of snuck up on a guy. And she hadn't been kidding about her love of lavender, either. Where most people had shrubs for landscaping, she had monster plants. Interspersed with those were other flowers and some large pieces of pottery that reminded him of her mother's stuff from Provence.

"Mom and I don't go for small souvenirs," she said as he ran his fingers around the rim of a tall, deep blue urn on her front porch.

"Not carry-on for sure," he said, waiting for her to open her screen door and unlock the bright red door that sat behind it.

"Move it along, Howard," she said to a cat he could hear yowling just inside the door. Good thing he liked cats, since Howard sounded like the type who demanded attention.

"Come on in," she said to him.

Steve stepped inside, and once again his world turned upside down. Based on her career and clothing choices, he'd expected to find a practical place—modern decor, maybe, with stacks of books tucked into a giant bookcase. What he stepped into, though, was like a sexy garden of deep greens, pale golds and bright sunlight. Howard, who looked exactly as smug as Steve had expected, sat as a pitch-black counterpoint on the hardwood floor.

"Interesting, professor," he said as he took in an old piece of garden statuary occupying one corner. The shape was that of Venus, but her lower face was obscured by a harem veil. Unable to help himself, he walked over and lifted the gauzy fabric. It seemed that Venus's chin had gone missing.

"She was out in the trash, as though one tumble meant she was no good," Sarah said. "I couldn't stand the waste."

Steve would bet that more than waste had spurred the reclamation of Venus. He saw a little empathy and a whole lot of passion in the project. He shook his head as he imagined her wrestling the concrete Venus up her front steps. Sarah Stanton was as tough as her mother, just in a very different way. He wondered if Sarah had any idea exactly how amazing she was.

"What?" she asked. "Is something wrong?"

"Nope."

"Then I'll just assume you're giving me that weird look for sport."

"It's called admiration, Sarah."

She shook her head as though she must have misheard him. "Right. Well, this is my house, offbeat as it is. I wanted it to be a retreat from the business I deal with all day, but I didn't want to waste money, either."

"Very sensible," he replied, barely managing to keep a straight face. How she managed daily to cloak her passion and sensuality from the outside world without exhausting herself was beyond him. And how he'd go another minute without taking her in his arms and feeling her warmth against his body was beyond him, too.

"Back this way is the kitchen," she said, gesturing at an archway leading to a hall. "And the laundry room, a bathroom, and my office are back there, too." She stepped around Howard and pointed to the stairway. "Upstairs, there used to be three bedrooms, but I opened a wall between the two smallest to make a bigger master bedroom. There's nothing like knocking down plaster to take the edge off a day's frustrations."

"That's one approach," he said.

Color had risen on her face, not so much a blush as

what he hoped was a heightened awareness of him…and his growing hunger to kiss her. He came closer, but she retreated a step.

"I'm thirsty. Are you thirsty?" she asked in a cheery voice.

"Yes," he replied even though he really wasn't. She needed her space, and he would give it to her.

"Have a seat," she said, pointing to a fat, silvery-green sofa with a wild paisley throw draped across its upper contours. "I'll get us something to drink and be right back." She turned away, but just as quickly turned back. "Water? Sun tea? Soda?"

"Sun tea sounds good."

She nodded, then headed down the hallway to the kitchen.

Though Steve was tempted to check out the photos above the fireplace, he didn't want her to come back in and find him snooping, so he settled on the sofa. Howard jumped up beside him, close enough to investigate but not so close that his curiosity might be mistaken for a loss of feline aloofness. Funny how that drew attention the cat's way all the faster. And sad how much more complicated matters were for humans.

"Dude, you don't know how easy you've got it," he said to the cat, and he took the cat's twitch of long whiskers as an answering "Don't you know it?"

Steve hunkered down to wait.

SARAH, WHO WAS NOT IN THE least thirsty, stood in front of her open refrigerator staring at the jar of sun tea as though it might be an oracle about to dispense the advice she so sorely needed. Because she was a sensible woman, she knew all she'd be getting was orange pekoe.

She pulled the jar from the fridge and sat it on the counter, then opened the cupboard above the sink to pull out two of the tall glasses she'd picked up in an antique shop in Savannah the prior Christmas—and after a round of haggling, for a very good deal, too.

Hands braced on the counter and head tipped downward, Sarah tried to get a grip. How the heck could she be so calm and assertive in her daily life and yet such a wimp when it came to matters of the heart?

Since the glasses were both too tall and delicate for her ice dispenser, she grabbed a plastic cup and filled that with ice, then transferred it. As she poured the tea and then returned the jar to the fridge, she considered how to best go into the living room and tell Steve that she would very much like to make love with him. Sure, it was a more personal question than 'Would you like sugar in your tea?'—which she'd forgotten to ask—but it was hardly insurmountable for a woman with her life experience.

So why did the question feel so ridiculously huge? And why were her palms sweaty?

Sarah abandoned the tea and stepped into the bathroom, thinking that a little dab of the lavender oil she kept in there might calm her. She switched on the light and caught her own reflection in the mirror, generally not a good idea for a woman smack in the middle of a crisis of confidence. Except she looked…*good*. Her emotional agitation seemed to have given her a little color, but not too much. And her hair, which had just the wrong amount of natural curl, seemed to be working.

So even if she didn't have her act together on the inside, the outside was cruising along. And if she didn't take this risk today, she'd be kicking herself tomorrow, and no doubt for many days to follow.

"Suck it up and get out there," she said to herself.

"Are you talking to me?" Steve called from the front room.

Darned small house. Every sound carried.

"No," she called back. No need to point out that she'd been talking to herself. He could do the math.

Sarah turned off the light and went back to the kitchen for the tea.

She could and would do this.

"Here you go," she said to Steve, placing one glass on the low cocktail table in front of the sofa. She remained standing and took at least a ceremonial sip of her own.

"I wasn't really thirsty," she said. "I'm plenty nervous, though. I don't generally have men to my house."

He smiled. "I'll put that on the good news side of the list, then."

She didn't know he'd been list-keeping.

"And on the bad news side?" she asked.

"That we live a continent apart seems to be the only item at this point. I'm sure more will come, though."

This didn't sound good. "Such as?"

He frowned, but she could see the laughter in his blue eyes. "I don't know…. Do you maybe have a secret obsession with collecting knives?"

She laughed aloud. "No."

"No ex-boyfriends buried beneath the lavender bushes?"

"None worth mentioning," she replied in the teasing spirit of the moment.

"Then I can't think of a single additional item for that list." He patted the couch cushion, earning a ticked-off look from Howard. "Could you could come and sit by me?"

She shooed her cat, put her glass next to Steve's untouched one, then sat. Still, she couldn't relax enough to lean against the couch's back cushion.

"Thank you for inviting me into your house," he said. "I'm honored. Really."

"And you're welcome…literally. At least, thus far you are."

He laughed. "Thanks for the glowing endorsement."

"I try. But as long as we're asking questions, any ex-girlfriends in empty wine barrels?"

"Not a one. They're all still living and breathing, and most of them I consider friends."

It was now or never.

"Well, in that case…"

She moved closer and brushed a brief and teasing kiss against his mouth. But once she was that close, the temptation to linger eased into her bones, banishing the last of her hesitancy and drawing her even closer yet.

Yes, he was definitely worth the risk.

ONE OF THE GOOD THINGS ABOUT being fifty was that Steve no longer felt compelled to prove he could be amorous and acrobatic at the same time. If he were still a raw youth, he'd be trying to figure out how to make love to Sarah then and there, working her out of her prim outfit and yet at the same time not sending those glasses of iced tea just inches away tumbling onto the floor.

At fifty, he liked beds—big, not-too-soft ones—and privacy, even from a cat named Howard. And at fifty, it seemed he liked secretly sexy professors one whole helluva lot.

"That bedroom of yours?" he murmured.

"Mmm-hmm?" She looked dazed and dewy and absolutely adorable.

"Do you think I could persuade you to take me up to see it?"

Her mouth curved into a knowing smile. "I could be persuaded."

Damn, but he loved being teased by her just as much as he loved teasing her.

"Let's see how this works," he said, then kissed her long and deep and hard, until they were both breathless. And then he tipped her chin up so that their eyes could meet. He wondered if he looked as wowed as she did. He sure as heck felt it.

Sarah took his hand and pressed a kiss against his palm.

"I'd say that did the job," she announced.

Fingers still locked with his, she rose. Steve had to smile at the way she'd staggered a little.

He came to his feet, concentrating on making a body with one very strong imperative—make love, now!—follow basic commands like *stand* and *think*.

"Just to get the rest of the awkwardness out of the way...I have protection," she said.

"I do, too," he said, thankful that he'd optimistically loaded his wallet with more than cash. "But I want you to know something more. You're safe with me. Your heart, all of you...you'll always be safe with me."

"Thank you," she said.

Despite her words, he could see the lingering doubt in her tentative expression. He couldn't blame her. They had an undeniable attraction toward each other, they shared laughter and a curiosity about the world, but what they truly knew of each other was outdistanced by what they didn't. For him, going with instinct was easy and natural. He could see that wasn't true for Sarah.

Something had happened in her life to make her close her true self away, using only this house as an outlet for her originality. He knew she'd been married twice, and he knew from personal experience that divorce was hell. But there was more behind the shadows in her eyes and her intentionally plain exterior. The knowledge that she'd take this risk to let him in made him all the more determined to earn her trust.

And as she clasped his hand tighter and led him upstairs, he vowed he'd make this damn good for both of them.

NIGHT HAD FULLY FALLEN, AND SARAH slept upstairs with such utter peacefulness that it had been difficult for Steve to leave her. In nothing but his jeans and bare feet, he'd padded to the rental car to retrieve his travel bag. It was pretty clear that he'd be staying with Sarah and not Dean and Patsy tonight.

And because that was the case, he now sat in her living room, cell phone in hand. It was time to tell his original hosts that he was going to be a no-show. Steve hit the autodial number for Dean's cell phone.

"Hey," he said when Dean answered.

"Get delayed coming into town?" his friend asked.

"No. I'm here."

"Not at my house, you're not, or someone other than Milo would be having a beer with me right now."

Milo was Dean's granddad and had raised him after Dean's parents had died in an accident. The old curmudgeon was into his early nineties and had no intention of slowing down. Steve hoped that he and Dean would be just the same way.

"It looks like it's going to be just the two of you tonight," Steve said.

"You've made other arrangements?" Dean asked.

"Yeah."

Dean was no dummy. He knew exactly what was going on.

"She's not your usual type," Dean said.

"And?"

"And…I don't know. Just that I like her and I love you like a brother so I hope this makes you happy and that you don't tick off Patsy when this ends."

Which was pretty much enough male sharing for one night.

"Good enough," Steve said. "We'll both see you around noon for the party, then? Can I bring anything?"

"Your appetite. Patsy and Juliana haven't left the kitchen in the past twenty-four hours."

Steve laughed. "So I should expect the customary Grosso eat-until-you-die food spectacular?"

"You got it, buddy. See you tomorrow."

Steve hung up and then set his cell phone on the cocktail table next to two very warm glasses of formerly iced tea. Maybe it was his lack of sleep or maybe it was just because he was surrounded in Sarah's belongings with her scent still lingering on his skin and her touch in his memory, but he was having strange thoughts.

Very strange.

He hadn't been part of an official couple in almost a decade, when one of the original chicklets had ditched him for some Irish punk guitarist. And he'd been happy with his single yet date-filled existence. Now, though, he could see the appeal of having someone who knew him in a way the chicklets never could.

And more than that, he could see the appeal of Sarah. Earlier, he had joked with her about keeping a list, but if he were to keep one, it was all winning points.

She "got" him; he wasn't just someone good to be seen with. She wasn't beside him because he'd been a champion driver and she didn't seem to care about his relative wealth.

Sarah and he were of an age, too. He bet if he made a reference to Jimmy Carter with any of the chicklets, all he'd get in return was a perky and ever-so-blank smile in response. Sarah would no doubt want to analyze the entire post-Watergate era. He liked that. A lot.

She was also so busy with her own career that she likely wouldn't grow to resent the time that Pebble Valley and his travels on its behalf consumed. He had money enough that he could fly her in for long weekends and travel here, too. Plus, he could see taking a lazy summer, someday, to explore Europe with her. To him, the continent was a series of airports and meeting rooms. There was so much he wanted to see, and he'd get a real kick out of having her at his side.

And then there was the deal clincher. While Sarah was still of childbearing age, she was nearing the edge of the envelope. He couldn't imagine her wanting kids and not having had them by now. She was too determined to have passed that up unintentionally. As for him, he'd had Mattie, and that was enough. He regretted the lingering disconnect that was the product of his endless weeks on the road with her at home, but he couldn't have done it any other way. Now, that time in his life had passed, and he could see filling the coming days with Sarah.

"Think you could learn to share a little?" he asked Howard, who lurked at the base of the stairs.

The cat gave a flick of his tail and then ambled across the room to sit beside Steve. He ran his hand down the cat's silken back and chuckled.

"This could be the beginning of a beautiful friendship."

SARAH'S BED WAS EMPTY OF A LOVER. Yes, this was its usual state, but she had just discovered that she much preferred having one particular lover in it: Steve. She stretched her limbs and snuggled under the covers, smiling as she thought about how wonderful it had been to make love with him. Once her initial nerves had passed, she'd allowed herself to live in the moment, to feel and love and be loved in return. The act could be downright habit-forming.

Love.

That wasn't a word that Sarah bandied about. She loved her mother fiercely. She loved her friends; the few she had were very close, but she was hesitant to let others in. And, yes, she loved Martin with great devotion, but she hadn't been *in* love with him for a very long time…if ever. After Martin's and ex number two's betrayals, she had learned to hold her heart closely. And not once over the years had she met a man worth the risk of that safety.

But Steve was different. It wasn't so much that he was from a different background. She could filter out the glamour, the looks, the nearly universal appeal, and still he was different. In a good way, too.

With Steve, there were no games. She had the feeling that he said what he meant, and how she felt about those words and what she did with them would be up to her. He wouldn't lie, and she was safe.

And she was very much afraid that she was beginning to fall in love with him.

Sarah wished for a best girlfriend to talk to, but considering whom she worked with, it was no surprise that her best friends were guys. She could talk to them about a lot of things, but sex, which had been fabulous, and budding love, which apparently had made for fabulous sex, weren't on the chat list.

She cringed at the thought of discussing these new feelings with her mother. Mom would be torn between laughter and lecture, and she would feel more naked than she was at this moment.

That left Martin, who would die a thousand deaths to know that she'd even been thinking of him in the context of "best girlfriend." And in any case, he'd treated her like a child this afternoon. She wasn't game for an encore.

Just then, she heard Steve padding upstairs. In a weird moment of panic, Sarah wanted to flee, but stilled herself, instead. She could talk to him about her feelings, but she knew from her guy friends' date dissections that would be dating suicide this early on. She could feign sleep, the standard coward's way out. Or…

"I've missed you," she said as Steve entered the bedroom.

Why not create another memory for after he was gone?

CHAPTER EIGHT

MAYBE IT WAS THE SCANT TEN hours of sleep over the past two days. Maybe it was the triumphant/smug laugh and hug that Patsy had given him when he and Sarah had reached the Grosso farm's front door. Or maybe it was the fact that sometime over the past twenty hours his life had changed and Steve was feeling behind the curve. Whatever. The bottom line was that he wanted a cold glass of wine and a private corner to kick back in. The wine, he'd grab for himself. The privacy was nowhere to be found in this crew.

Patsy had hijacked Sarah to the kitchen, even after Sarah had laughingly explained that she cooked three dishes well and otherwise stuck to carry-out. He was sure that Sarah's time among the extended clan of Grosso women would be occupied by questions and more questions, and not food prep. After having witnessed her mother's luncheon table, he was also sure that Sarah could handle it.

Steve slipped through the family room and out to the large back terrace, where Dean was at a new grill approximately the size of a car. Along the way to the grilling action, he snagged a glass of Pebble Valley Chardonnay.

"Grab some tongs and flip a few birds with me," Dean said.

The chickens looked about the size of quail on the enormous grill grate. Damn thing was, Steve would have to get one this size once he was back in Sonoma. He'd hated being outraced, and now he hated being outgrilled.

"Interesting grill," he said while bringing a bird breast side up.

Dean laughed. "Yeah. Patsy said if we go bust, we can always move into it for our retirement home."

He imagined that practical Patsy had said one heck of a lot more than that when the new grill had arrived.

"Meetings in Sonoma go okay?" Dean asked after a swig of his beer.

"They were worth the trip home and then some. I have a new business partner, assuming the lawyers don't screw up our deal. His name's Tieri and he was a hedge fund manager in New York City."

Dean chuckled. "Back when being a hedge fund manager was cool, I'll bet."

"He's out now, and with lots of cash to invest," Steve said. "I think this is going to work."

Dean's skepticism was written across his face. "You've never been the kind of guy to partner up easily…in any aspect of your life."

"Yeah, well, there's never been the right incentive to do it. Tieri's money is big incentive, but the fact that he'll leave me to the wine and look after the marketing makes him even more my kind of partner."

"So long as it works for you, that's all that matters," Dean said.

"It does," Steve said, then had a swallow of his wine. Damn good, if he didn't say so himself.

Dean glanced over his shoulder, then barked out an order to Kent to go see if his mother had anything else that needed to be on the grill right away. After a friendly wave to Steve, Kent went to it. Dean's son might have been wealthy and a champion in his own right, but in the Grosso household he was still a kid who took marching orders with no guff. Steve wished for less guff from Mattie, but he might as well also wish for pigs to fly.

He checked out the crowd for a glimpse of his daughter, but she wasn't to be found. No shock. She'd always had a way of sneaking up on him.

"So, speaking of partnering, where's Sarah?" Dean asked.

"In the kitchen with your wife."

"Could be dangerous," Dean said.

"The thought had occurred, but it would be more dangerous for me to go in there."

"True. So things are good with Sarah?" Dean asked.

Last night, he would have admitted to it. After the minefield of a conversation he and the professor had shared over breakfast this morning, he was admitting to nothing. Except that last night had been incredible, which Dean didn't need to know.

"Think I'll go top off my wine," he said to his friend.

Dean shot him a quick grin. "No comment? Tough break for Sarah. Another one bites the dust...."

Except this time Steve suspected that he was the one going down.

PACKED TO THE CABINETS WITH WOMEN, the Grosso kitchen surfed an estrogen buzz. Sarah had to laugh when Kent refused to come any closer than three inches inside the door to see if more food required grilling, and then escaped like a condemned man spotting an escape route. As for Sarah, she was enjoying the loving banter that surrounded her.

"Gently, or you'll bruise the strawberries!" Juliana Grosso said to Patsy's daughter Sophia, whom Sarah had just met.

Sophia looked up from the berries she was hulling. "I'm a nurse. I'll tend them if I do."

Sarah ducked her head to hide her smile.

"Sarah, come out to the herb garden with me. We need more fresh basil for the insalata caprese," Patsy said loudly enough for Juliana to give a firm "get to it" nod as they slipped from the kitchen.

The trip through the family room was an extended one. It seemed with every couple of steps there were more people Patsy wanted Sarah to meet. By the time they'd reached the patio, Sarah swore she'd met every parts supplier for Cargill-Grosso Racing, as well as half of NASCAR's administration.

"Being able to deal with throngs of people is a prerequisite around here," Patsy said once they'd finally made it to the terrace.

"Oh, I'm used to throngs of people," Sarah replied. "Except I'm usually standing at the front of the lecture hall and they're obediently sitting in their seats."

"Not so much obedience at Villa Grosso," Patsy said. "Take, for example, Dean and the grill that ate North Carolina. He had that brought in and assembled while we were in New Hampshire. Smart man, since I would have sent it to the scrapyard for recycling had I seen it arrive."

She waved in the direction of Dean and Steve, who stood together by the biggest accumulation of stainless steel that Sarah had seen outside a science lab. Dean waved back, and Steve saluted with his wineglass. If Sarah were forced to pick one word for Steve's expression, she'd have to choose cranky. In fact, he'd been that way since awakening. Not that they'd slept much.

"What's the matter with Steve?" Patsy asked as they took the broad stone steps down to a lower terrace that was ringed with raised herb beds.

"He missed naptime," Sarah replied with just a nip of spice. "And apparently he needs it or his whole day goes south."

Patsy laughed. "Trouble in paradise?"

"It could be a short detour on the way to paradise, as I can't say I've been there yet." Except maybe last night.

Patsy began pinching basil leaves and putting them in the bowl she'd carried from the kitchen. Sarah joined in the ritual, too.

"I love Steve," Patsy said.

Funny, because I'm beginning to think I might, too.
Not quite the response one could give to one of Steve's best friends, so she said nothing.

"Really, he's been in my life nearly as long as Dean. But I have to say this, until he started looking at you, I thought he'd never catch on to what a real woman could bring into his life."

"If, by real, you mean I'm all original parts, you're right. But as for the rest of it, I'm not sure I'm bringing anything much to either of us. Witness the grumpy act by the grill," Sarah said. "And all because I didn't want to commit to staying with him in Daytona."

Patsy stopped plucking basil and turned her full attention to Sarah. "Wait. He actually asked you to stay with him? In his suite?"

"Yes."

"And you told him no?"

"I'm not ready for all of this togetherness. I need to prepare myself for it."

Patsy waved that comment off. "Strange, but we'll deal with it later. I don't suppose Steve mentioned that he never—and I do mean *never*—has anyone stay with him while he's on the road? He's quite private."

"Really? I find that tough to reconcile with his public image."

"That's just it. Some men, say, like Dean, are comfortable in the public eye. Others, like Steve, do just that…they craft a public image. With Steve, he just throws out more smiles and turns up the Hollywood wattage. People are blinded by that, and he knows it. He uses it to control public situations."

Sarah suspected she'd seen some of that yesterday, especially when Martin had been acting less than gracious.

"And he's always used his downtime to recharge... *alone.* Even if he has someone with him, they have their own room."

"Ah."

"Yes, *ah.* That's why I'm surprised...and really quite impressed that he's asked you to join him," Patsy said, then turned back to collecting basil.

Sarah rubbed one of the leaves between her fingers, then inhaled the pungent fragrance. It wasn't quite lavender, but it provided her with a distraction as she sorted through her feelings. But no matter how many times she sorted, *scared* and *cautious* kept coming out at the top of the pile. And yet Steve was willing to go all out for her. Sarah added a pinch of slightly guilty to her emotional mix.

"I doubt his invitation will be repeated very soon," she said.

Patsy laughed. "Oh, don't be so sure. Steve doesn't hear the word *no* often. I'm certain it's making him all the more determined."

"And cranky," Sarah added.

With basil leaves aplenty, Sarah and Patsy returned to the upper terrace.

"It looks as though you're about to meet another Clayton," Patsy said. "See the girl with dark hair and a sassy look on her face heading this way?"

"Yes?"

"That's Steve's daughter, Mattie."

Sarah searched for a means of escape. "I think I'll…ah…" But it was too late. Mattie Clayton moved with as much speed and purpose as her father.

"Aunt Patsy, it's been too long," the younger woman said as she approached.

Patsy handed Sarah the basil bowl before wrapping Mattie in a hug.

"It has," Patsy said, then gave Mattie a kiss on the cheek before stepping back. "We've all missed you. Your father's here…over by the grill with Uncle Dean."

Mattie nodded. "And they were my very first stop."

She looked curiously at Sarah, who worked up a polite smile. Obviously, Steve hadn't mentioned her to his daughter. On the whole, Sarah was fine with that.

"Mattie," Patsy said, "I'd like you to meet a friend of mine, Sarah Stanton. Sarah's a professor at Larchmont College. She's traveling with us to races for the next several weeks since she's about to move into the motorsports management program."

Mattie held out her hand. Sarah switched the basil bowl to her left hand and shook Mattie's.

"It's nice to meet you," Sarah said.

"So what do you think of all this NASCAR fun?" Mattie asked.

"I'm loving it!"

Mattie smiled. "Great. I'm glad you have Aunt Patsy and Uncle Dean to show you around. I can't think of anyone better."

Except maybe your father, Sarah could have said, but didn't. She glanced over at Steve, who was looking their way with a tight expression. There were countless possibilities for that, so she decided not to take it personally.

"Where's Kent?" Mattie asked Patsy.

"I'm sure he and Tanya are somewhere nearby."

"Probably joined at the hip still, too." She wrinkled her nose. "Newlyweds. Can't figure out what would make a perfectly good couple run off and get married."

Patsy laughed. "Your day will come, sweetheart, and I can't wait to see it."

"You'll be waiting a good, long while." Mattie looked to the other side of the terrace, where someone was calling her name. "Hey, it was nice to meet you, Sarah. Maybe our paths will cross again."

"Maybe," Sarah agreed genially.

And with that, Mattie Clayton was gone.

Patsy gave a rueful shake of her head. "If you look up *headstrong* in the dictionary, you'll see a photo of Mattie."

"Better that than not being able to stand up for herself," Sarah said.

"No risk of that in the Clayton gene pool," Patsy replied with a laugh. "And now we'd better get ourselves back to the kitchen before Juliana calls out the troops to find us."

STEVE LIKED COOKOUTS. Really, between grilled meat and chilled wine, what wasn't to like? Except the fact that he and his purported date had been circling each other like combatants in a sparring match. He'd cooked while she'd helped inside, then she'd talked with Patsy like they were lifelong friends, while he'd caught up with Mattie. Actually, it had been more Mattie catching him up. The girl had allowed only a scant few syllables of agreement.

Now that most of the guests had been served, Steve planned to sit and eat, and he'd be damned if he'd do it with anyone other than Sarah. He met up with her at the buffet table, which was laden Grosso-style with a wealth of food. He looked at Sarah's plate and was pleased to see that she wasn't one of those women who feigned having no appetite.

"Have an issue with my choices?" she asked.

"None at all. Do you think maybe we could try eating together?"

She scrutinized him the way he had her meal selection. "Does food improve your mood?"

"Usually."

"In that case, here." She plopped a scoop of potato salad onto the one empty spot he had left on his plate.

He laughed. "You, professor, are a gem."

"And you, Steve Clayton, can be a total crank."

"True enough, but luckily it doesn't happen often. So, will you eat with me?"

"I will," she replied.

"Good."

As nearly the last to dine, they ended up squeezing in down at Dean and Patsy's end of the long, communal table. Steve and Dean traded talk about the upcoming Daytona race, and as Sarah asked some very smart questions, Steve's mood improved. Apparently a good meal could be trumped by the company of a smart woman. Just then, another smart woman joined them—his daughter.

"Do you mind?" Mattie asked as she gestured at the bit of bench that was open next to Sarah.

"Of course not," Sarah replied.

Steve might have answered otherwise, judging by the curve to one corner of Mattie's mouth. From childhood, she'd gotten that very look when in a rabble-rousing mood.

Sarah moved down as much as she could, so now instead of having her directly across from him, he faced the duo of daughter and not-quite-girlfriend.

"So, Dad, you didn't bring a date, or maybe she's out taking her road test for her driver's license?" Mattie asked. "That sweet sixteen is a big year, you know."

Yeah, she was wearing that smile for a reason. She'd always loved getting under his skin. It was only after she'd gone off to college that he'd understood why she'd done it. Often, it had been the only way she could get his attention. Not true now, but old habits died hard…if at all.

"Funny, kid," Steve said, and was mid-topic-change with Sarah when Mattie cut in.

"Really, I don't see a chicklet in sight."

"Chicklet?" Sarah asked.

"My dad has interesting taste in women. Young women. *Very* young women. I live in fear that one day I'll have a stepmother younger than I am." She gave Sarah the once-over. "Are you married?"

"No," she replied.

"Have you ever been?"

"On occasion."

"On occasion…I like that. Hey, Dad, think I should pass that answer on to my mother? I think four times is 'on occasion'…actually, many occasions."

Steve let his scowl do the talking, not that Mattie was focusing on him at the moment. She'd angled herself for a clear view of Sarah.

"I like you," she was saying. "You're smart and have a good sense of humor…. I don't suppose you have a daughter my dad can date?"

"Enough, Matilda," Steve commanded. Use of her full name should have stopped her, but Mattie was on a roll.

"The last chicklet, I think Hef has her up at the Playboy mansion now."

"Really. Enough. I don't pry into your social life, and I'd appreciate the same in return, okay? And Lexi is not at the Playboy mansion." He didn't think it would help his case to say that, actually, she was under lockdown on a reality show in England.

"Sure thing, Dad. But no chicklet to marry means that I won't get the little sister I keep asking Santa for. What's a girl to do?"

Steve would have said "Have a kid of your own" but no way was he ready to be a grandfather.

"Sorry, sweetheart," he replied instead. "You did me in for kids…forever."

Mattie smiled. "I was just the girl for the job, too, wasn't I?"

He took a look at Sarah, who was acting enthralled

by her food, except she was just nudging it with her fork instead of actually eating.

Yeah, Mattie was the girl for the job. And then some.

USUALLY, SARAH APPRECIATED humor; it lessened the sting in many painful situations. She knew that she was witnessing nothing more than some harmless kidding between father and daughter, but to her it felt as harmless as glass shards being planted under her fingernails.

Logic—one of her very best tools—compelled that she not be upset. Steve's daughter had no way of knowing that her father had ventured from the land of chicklets into that of fully adult women. All the same, it rankled Sarah to think that Mattie couldn't envision her father involved with her. Maybe she wasn't surgically enhanced and had lived a few years, but if one were to measure wrinkle-for-wrinkle and year-for-year against Steve, she was looking pretty darned good! She knew her worth.

But beneath that silly surface stuff—the things she could and would discard as not meaningful—ran a deeper feeling of alarm. She wanted a child very much. To hear someone she was growing to love say that he was done with children, even in a joking fashion, didn't sit well.

Sarah pushed a bit of grilled red pepper around with her fork as she tried to get her emotions tucked back away. Hypersensitivity wasn't going to cut it. She tried to act engaged in the conversation drifting around her, one that had moved on to teasing by Patsy about Dean's need for a "see me!" grill, and his challenge to Steve to try to out-do that.

Reprieve came in the form of Tanya Grosso stopping by to help clear plates, and Patsy and Dean rising to join her.

"Let me help, too," Sarah volunteered.

Mattie rose to let her off the bench and gave her a friendly smile, a facsimile of which Sarah returned. In time, this stinging would pass. In time, she'd be Common Sense Sarah. Just not right this second...

CHAPTER NINE

A PEACEFUL COOKOUT...was that too much to ask? Steve was beginning to think so. He gave Mattie one last glare for good measure.

"What?" she asked. "Am I about to be grounded?"

"Wish I could," Steve muttered.

"You weren't so good at it, even back when."

True story.

Mattie was looking around the crowd in a way that set off further alarms.

"What's up?" he asked.

"I'd like a few minutes with Dean and Patsy."

"Here? In the middle of their party?"

"In case you haven't noticed, they're always in the middle of something."

Also a true story. "Is this work or personal stuff?"

"I didn't know you cared."

"Of course I do. Save the flip attitude for an audience, okay?"

"Point taken," she said. "It's a mix of work and personal, Dad. I've tripped over some information about Gina's disappearance." She shook her head. "This is all so strange, to even find out that I might have another cousin of sorts out there. Why didn't anyone ever talk about her when we were kids?"

"It was a tough time, Mattie. Your godparents went through a lot, losing Gina. It's not as though we ever forgot, or didn't grieve. It was just time to let the hurt drift off."

"I understand," Mattie replied. "And I feel horrible for Aunt Patsy and Uncle Dean. But now, if there's some chance I can help find Gina or at least what really happened to her, I want to help." She shook her head. "Actually, I *need* to help."

Steve knew that his daughter was acting with the very best of intentions. He also knew that sometimes her passion got in the way of her people skills. He'd been guilty of that in his youth, too.

"Patsy has plenty of people helping her already, including a cousin of hers named Jake McMasters, who's a private investigator. How about if I get you in contact with him?"

She shook her head. "No way. I have things I need to tell her."

"I'm not going to try to talk you out of this, but I am going to come with you," he said. "You're dangerous today."

"What do you mean, dangerous?"

"I mean that you have on your 'I'm gonna rock the world' attitude, and you've rocked it plenty already."

She tilted her head, and a lock of her dark hair fell over her eyes. She impatiently brushed it away. "Really? How?"

"For starters, I came here with Sarah Stanton. I'm, ah, seeing her."

"Seeing her, as in dating her?"

"Yes."

"Wow! No sh—"

"Mattie!"

"Sorry, you shook me, there." She sat silent for a second. "I really put my foot in it, with that date-your-daughter joke, and she seems nice, too. Should I go apologize?"

Steve shook his head. "No. Let's just let it fade into the evening, okay?" He was sure he was going to catch chicklet hell from Sarah, in any case.

Mattie popped to her feet. "I'm going to go help in the kitchen for a few minutes. Do you think you could round up Uncle Dean for me? I could use you in the room, anyway. You're good at keeping me anchored…when I let you."

"Sure, I can find him," Steve said.

Though he ascribed to Dean's school of "Let's allow the past to rest," he knew that there was no stopping these events. At the very least he could soften them, as Dean and Patsy had done for him so many times.

"How about if we meet in the library in about ten minutes?"

Mattie nodded. "Deal." And then she was gone.

Steve finished his glass of wine and surveyed the empty seats around him. Maybe next year he'd get his peaceful picnic.

THE VILLA GROSSO LIBRARY was nearly as much a museum as that at Cargill-Grosso Racing, though in a much more personal way. Racing trophies sat cheek to jowl with framed childhood artwork created by Grosso children years earlier, and fading color photos of holidays long passed. For Steve, the room created a sense of home and peace.

He wished that he had more of this in his life. Oh, he had the trophies, but he came up short on the personal items…sketches Mattie might have made, or photos of his mom and him. When Pebble Valley's business leveled out, he'd see if he could get Rosita to help him unearth some of this stuff and get it ready for display. Of course, he could recall thinking this same thought every time he'd been in this room, and yet his library remained as impersonal as ever.

"Want to give me a little forewarning of what's about to go down?" Dean asked.

"Mattie has come up with some information on Gina that she wants to share."

Dean, who was sitting on one of the two fat leather sofas, tipped back his head and stared at the ceiling for a moment, then looked back to Steve.

"Any chance you can make her drop this for the day, at least? Patsy's been so relaxed and having such a good time. I don't want to see it end."

"I know," Steve said. "But we both know Mattie. Once she has a mission, she's going to see it through."

"I can't blame her. You know, that's the killer of this whole mess. Since talk of Gina's disappearance has resurrected itself, I've spent just as many sleepless nights as Patsy. The difference is, I worry about Patsy, too. I'm torn between wanting to know about Gina and not seeing Patsy suffer any more. Odds are this isn't going to end well, Steve."

"I know," he said.

Dean's sigh was heavy. "But it has to end."

The library door opened, and Patsy came in with Mattie on her heels.

Patsy sat next to Dean and said, "Mattie has something she'd like to talk to us about."

"So I've been told," Dean replied. "What's up, Mattie?"

"I don't quite know how to start this, so I'm just going to jump in," she said.

No shock there, Steve thought.

"I've been down in Naples, Florida, talking to a retired doctor who worked in the hospital where Kent and Gina were born."

Patsy edged forward on the sofa. "And?"

"This Jim has dropped word here and there that he believes he knows what might have happened to Gina."

"Really?" Dean asked, sounding skeptical at best.

"He was in his last couple of weeks before an overseas assignment when he began to notice a nurse… not one of the staff, but a temp, who was acting strangely," Mattie said. "He was pretty busy, wrapping up things there and getting ready for his move, so he said that it had to be something really unusual to stick in his mind. It seemed to him that this nurse was always there, hovering over the babies, and not in a good way. In fact, he used the word *lurking* when he described it to me."

"When was this?" Patsy asked. "Were Kent and Gina in the nursery then?"

"No, he left a couple of weeks prior to their arrival."

"So this could mean nothing at all," Dean said. "It's just the recollection of a weirdly hovering nurse by one doctor who now must be getting old if he's retired."

Mattie shook her head. "He's not all that old, Uncle Dean, and he sure seemed to recall the feeling the woman left with him pretty clearly."

"And he never told the police about this?" Dean asked. "What makes you think this is a real lead?"

"See, that's the thing. He did tell the police once he'd heard from one of his friends stateside about the disappearance. But he didn't know the name of the woman, and didn't have any distinguishing physical characteristics that he could provide. I think that made the whole thing fizzle out."

"As it should have," Dean said.

Mattie shook her head. "That's not necessarily true. Sometimes it just takes that extra step."

"I agree," Patsy said. "What sort of parents would we be if we didn't follow up on every piece of information, no matter how small, that might lead us to Gina?"

Dean took Patsy's hand and wove her fingers through his own before kissing it. "Sweetheart, I understand how tough this is. Believe me, I do. But I can't stand the thought of you getting your hopes up only to have them crushed again."

"And I can't stand the thought of not knowing—*really* knowing—what happened to Gina. We have the resources to do this, Dean. Yes, it breaks my heart a little more each time a lead turns out to be nothing, but my heart will never be fully whole unless I do this. I need to call Jake…to have him follow up on all temporary nurses."

"It's pointless, Patsy," Dean said.

She pulled her hand from his and rose. "Can't you understand how much this means, and what we might gain in the way of peace?"

"I do. I just can't keep watching your pain and feeling so helpless. You follow up with Jake if you feel you need to, but at least understand why I don't feel the same need."

"I try, Dean Grosso. I try mightily, but sometimes…" She gave an impatient shake of her head. "Sometimes I just don't understand you at all."

As Patsy swept from the library, Steve reconsidered the piddling problems in his life. Maybe he and Sarah had yet to get their timing into sync, and maybe he needed to move it up a gear with Pebble Valley, but this kind of heartache he'd never experienced. He was one lucky, lucky man.

SARAH STOOD ON THE TERRACE chatting with a tire company exec she'd met in New Hampshire. The man was entertaining, in a throes-of-midlife-crisis sort of way, and she was glad that she'd secured some internship spots with his employer for her students. She did not, however, want to secure the dating spot for which he now seemed to be cautiously angling. At this moment, she wasn't entirely certain she ever wanted to date again.

Steve had been polite, finding her and telling her that he had to take care of a little business with his daughter. And she'd been equally gracious in return, but just now that seemed like hours ago. Eons, maybe. She nodded her head to something the tire man was saying. She had no idea what, so she hoped she hadn't just agreed to dinner in Daytona.

A hand settled low on her back, and Steve appeared beside her.

"Sorry I was gone so long," he said.

She gave him a bright smile, mostly for the tire man's benefit. "That's okay. You're here, now."

And with luck, he would also catch her silently telegraphed message of *Get me out of here, now!*

He looked at her and then at her conversation companion, then said, "Hey, Pat, you don't mind if I borrow Sarah for a few minutes? I promised to introduce her to Dean and Patsy's llamas today."

"Sure," the tire man said. "I'll see you later, then, Sarah?"

"In Daytona, I'm sure," she replied. "Take care!"

"Llamas?" she asked Steve as he led her off.

"They were the first things that came to my mind," he said.

"Scary."

"Patsy and Dean have them, if you're interested."

"I think I'd prefer the pond," she replied, pointing to

a wandering stone pathway that led to a beautifully landscaped water garden.

"Good enough," Steve replied.

They were nearly to the water's edge when he said to Sarah, "This day isn't turning out quite how I had envisioned it."

"You'd envisioned it?"

"Sure. I do with a lot of events in life. Races…buying the winery…"

They'd reached the pond. Sarah looked into the water where fat calico-colored koi swam expectantly, waiting for treats.

"So does that mean you envisioned the chicklets?" she asked.

He shook his head. "Do we really have to do this?"

"No. We could just agree on an amicable parting, and you could take me home."

"Not an option…at least, not on my end."

Sarah sat on a simple wooden bench just back from the pond's edge. "I wouldn't have raised the chicklets if I didn't want to understand what drives you. I don't like glossing over things, Steve. I need to really know."

"First, I'm not crazy about that term *chicklets,* okay? They're nice women and good for my business. And before you go getting all offended, I've been good for their business, too. Most of them want to be actresses or clothing designers, or…I don't know…just famous for no particular reason like a lot of people these days. Being seen with me gives them press, too."

He shook his head. "Okay, sorry. Wrong audience. I

should be telling all of that to Mattie. But in answer to your question, yes, I envisioned being seen with them, just not in the intimate way you're choosing to interpret."

"Okay," she said. "But it's shallow, Steve. Really, stupidly shallow to live like that. Do you have any idea how I felt when I ran your name through a search engine and—"

He held up one hand to stay her words. "Hang on. You looked me up on the Internet?"

"Of course I did. Do you think I'm a total dating idiot?"

He shook his head. "Unbelievable. So you knew about my dating habits even before Mattie launched her stand-up routine? I have never looked up a date beforehand."

"Then I suggest you join this century," she replied. "What if I were some sort of stalker?"

He laughed. "Fat chance. I've had one helluva time even getting you to be around me."

"Do you think maybe the Girl of the Week Club might have had something to do with that?"

"Well, now that I have some context here, yes."

"What is it you're looking for with me?" she asked. "Obviously, I've outlived my days as chicklet material. Even then, I would have had no desire to be trotted around like some man's pretty little show poodle. And I can't even begin to fathom why you'd be interested in doing that. It can't all be about the wine or the cars or whatever else you were busy promoting."

One hand on his hip, he looked down at the ground. She knew he was taking a moment to pull his words together, and had to appreciate that about him.

"Look, neither of us has been wildly successful in our personal lives, okay? I've met Martin, who is nice enough, but clearly managed to screw you over, somehow. I know you've been married once since then, but you won't even mention the guy's name."

"It might invoke evil spirits," she said, trying to joke her way past the sting that remained all these years later. He who must not be named had actually betrayed her with a close friend. Make that a formerly close friend.

Steve came and sat next to her. "I don't want to know what number two did, but if one day you decide to let me hunt down the bastard and shake a few of his teeth loose, I'm game, okay?"

He took her hand. "Until then, how about you understand that I'm well aware of my deficiencies in the relationship area, and I'm not really hot on having them given to me in a laundry list by a woman I've come to care about very much. Besides, I decided a few weeks ago that maybe it was time to remedy them."

"Really? When?"

He smiled. "When I was at a party in Sonoma. I saw this beautiful woman tapping away on her phone and ignoring all the activity around her."

"She's the weirdly focused sort," Sarah confided.

"So I've come to learn." He kissed the top of her hand. "How about if we both start looking forward, instead of back? How about if we figure out what we can be together instead of what we were—or weren't— with other people? And let's see how we do now before we begin to worry about the future."

Sarah didn't cry. At least, she didn't cry with any grace. And so she held back the silly tears she could feel waiting behind her eyes.

"I like who you are now…here, with me," she said to Steve. "I like you a whole lot."

"And I like you more than I have any woman in a very, very long time." He leaned back on the bench and looked out at the sky. "You know, if we stick around here until after sunset, we'll get to see fireworks."

Sarah smiled. "Let's say we go back to my house and make a few of our own."

CHAPTER TEN

"Too close to your skin color," Patsy said as Sarah held up the ivory-colored pantsuit she planned to pack for their Daytona trip, which was coming up that evening.

Patsy had called in the morning and decreed that they should have a packing party at the farm, followed by lunch out. Work and the pressure of the real world could wait for both of them. Sarah was all for it, since it fit in well with her extended vacation from reality…something that she and Steve had perfected the prior night.

So far, she'd witnessed the marvel that was Patsy's closet. It was an orderly and color-coordinated place, as Sarah would have expected from a woman who'd been a power in one of NASCAR's great racing families her entire adult life. It also spoke of Patsy's elegant style. She professed that she didn't like to dress up often, but she liked to do it well. Sarah could do worse for a fashion coach.

"And dressing in the same tone as your skin is a bad thing?" she asked her friend.

"Unless you want to look like a zombie on parade in photographs, it is."

Photographs. Visions of chicklets still danced in front of Sarah's eyes. They'd done that photo thing better than she could ever hope to. Still, she had to be practical. If she planned to ever walk in public with Steve Clayton, odds were good that she'd be photographed.

Sarah presented a khaki-colored version of the same suit. "Okay, how's this?"

Patsy flopped back on her bed, arms spread wide. "Do you own nothing with color to it?"

"Khaki *is* a color," Sarah said in defense of her favorite wear-it-anywhere shade.

"Barely. Do you have a dress packed in there?" Patsy asked.

"No, but I can't wear a dress to the race, anyway, right?"

"Correct. However, I heard Steve telling Dean that he's putting on a party and wine-tasting tomorrow night. Has he asked you to attend?"

"Yes. Actually, last night he asked me to cohost it with him."

Patsy grinned. "Did he, now? And what was your answer?"

Sarah conceded that it had been a yes.

"What do you plan to wear?"

"I don't know.… Khaki?"

Patsy sat up, then scooted off the bed to root through Sarah's suitcase herself. After a moment, she sighed in defeat.

"And you have nothing else at home?" she asked.

"One cat, one cat sitter and an empty closet. I know this might sound like blasphemy, but clothes just don't interest me. I find one thing I like and just get it in a couple of neutral colors."

"I'd rather be in jeans daily, but life doesn't always work that way," Patsy said, then flipped shut the top to Sarah's suitcase. "There's nothing to be done for it but to go shopping."

At that pronouncement, Sarah wanted to crawl into her travel bag and not come out. "I hate malls."

"Then we'll go to one of my favorite boutiques."

"Do they deliver?"

Patsy laughed. "They might, I've never asked. But I promise I'll make this as painless as possible. In and out, then on to lunch."

"Which elevates the idea only slightly above surgery with no anesthesia, but you're on."

And it had darned well better be worth it....

DAYTONA IN JULY WASN'T one of Steve's favorite climates. Humidity and he just didn't mix, one more reason he'd settled in Sonoma. And one more reason he'd chosen a well air-conditioned Italian nightclub beachside for this evening's Pebble Valley wines party. He'd had lots of heat last night, anyway.

After the quick hop down to Florida, he'd persuaded a very sleepy Sarah into his suite even though she had refused to give up her hotel room four floors down. And then he'd done the only thing a man could—made love to her. As it turned out, she was an early riser, just like him. They'd put the dawn to good use, too.

Today, though, he'd seen little of her. Patsy and she

had slipped away on some top secret errand just after breakfast. He'd spent the morning on the phone, then turned his attention to this party. The very one Sarah was supposed to be hosting with him, except she wasn't here and the doors were due to open in five minutes. He tried her cell phone one more time, but, like him, she seemed to believe in the "for my convenience, only" theory of cell ownership.

"Is there anything else we can do for you, Mr. Clayton?" the restaurant manager asked.

Steve checked out the arrangements, and they were just as he'd requested. White linens, tuxedoed waitstaff ready to circulate with trays of hors d'oeuvres, jazz quartet warming up by the dance floor and three tasting stations staffed by reps from his local distributors.

"It looks great, Samantha," he said. "Thank you."

The manager returned to the entry area and fussed with an arrangement of spiky tropical flowers. Steve looked at his watch yet again. The press was scheduled to be here in an hour. He'd had calls and text messages from various racing buddies and celebs who planned to drop by. All he needed was Sarah present and accounted for.

"I'm sorry, but we're not open quite yet," he heard the manager saying to someone who'd just entered.

"It's okay, we're good to go," he called, though apparently it hadn't been necessary.

"It's my fault," Patsy said as she and Sarah hustled past the hostess stand and into the restaurant. "Sarah asked me to keep track of time but I got distracted."

And Steve could see why.

Yes, that was Sarah next to Patsy, but one who shone more brightly. Her hair color was different, not startlingly so, but with more spark to it. Same with her features, all still simple and beautiful Sarah, but more noticeable, somehow. Now he could see the woman who'd created that Garden of Eden in which she lived. He quelled the urge to ask the manager to kick the air-conditioning up another notch, but, damn, suddenly he was feeling hot.

Sarah came forward, and because he couldn't help it, he gave her a fast, hard kiss.

"You look incredible," he said quietly, leaning close to her ear. "Amazing."

"It's still me," she said.

He brushed a kiss against her cheek. "And that's the very best part, as far as I'm concerned," he said and then stepped back to survey her.

"We've been having some fun," Patsy said. "Actually, lots of it."

Sarah smoothed her hands over her silky red dress. "Yesterday I discovered that I like shopping. Okay, maybe not *like,* but apparently I don't detest it, so we shopped more today. I think my credit card has gone into shock."

She did a modeling turn for him. "Like the dress? It's a wrap dress, which cracks me up because I can recall my mother wearing one of these in the 1970s."

He didn't care about who'd worn it so much as how enjoyable it was going to be to get her out of it. It skimmed her subtle curves in a way no man could miss.

"I've got the feeling that I like it more on you than I would Margaret," he said.

Sarah laughed. "Good. We wouldn't want to see you swinging too far the other way on the age continuum. Now is there anything I can do for you before the guests start arriving?"

"You mean in the next minute and a half?" he teased.

"Sorry. Pedicure," she said unrepentantly.

And then the rush began. Over the next three hours, Steve lost track of the number of hands he shook, bottles he signed and tastes he poured. He did, however, keep track of Sarah. She started out close to his side, but soon ventured off. He watched as she deftly moved from group to group, sharing talk and laughter with the guests. Plenty of guys were checking her out, too, but she didn't even seem to notice. She must have felt him watching her, though, because more than once she had looked his way, and they'd shared a smile. The night was better for it.

Patsy, who had been with Dean since he'd arrived, came to stand next to Steve.

"It looks like another Pebble Valley success," she said.

Steve nodded. "We have a lot of the local restaurateurs and specialty market owners here. My theory has always been that one taste will get us a follower, but it's tough building the business one taste at a time."

"Dean says you have a partner lined up. Will that mean more downtime for you?"

"At least more time in the vineyard, but, yes, probably a little more downtime."

She inclined her head in Sarah's direction. "Any chance you'll be sharing some of that with our friend?"

"I'd say there's a chance." An excellent one, so far as he was concerned.

"She looks incredible, doesn't she?"

"Definitely, but I want you to know that it hasn't been about appearances with Sarah."

"Really?" Patsy sounded surprised, and he supposed he deserved that.

"What I like most about Sarah comes from the inside…the way she looks at the world, her sense of humor…." He shook his head. "I can't explain it."

"It seems to me you're doing a pretty good job of explaining," Patsy said. "I'd give you my own take on what I'm seeing, but it would send you screaming into the night."

"Now that's a challenge I can't pass up. What's your take?"

She went up on tiptoe and whispered, "I think, Steve Clayton, that you have accidentally stumbled into a real relationship."

And Steve had no intention of stumbling back out.

"WHAT ARE YOU DOING UNDER the table, or dare I ask?" Martin said to Sarah as they shared a bistro lunch the Friday after she'd returned home from Daytona.

She glanced up at her friend. "I'm texting, though obviously I'm not quite as good at it as my students, or you wouldn't have caught me."

"Texting?"

"I'm answering a text message from Steve. It's our new thing."

"I wouldn't think you've been dating long enough to have had an old thing, let alone a new one," Martin said, then speared a potato from her Salad Nicoise.

She pulled her plate a little closer, feeling protective of her remaining carbohydrates.

Technically, she and Steve hadn't been together that long, but Steve had left behind neither speed nor determination when he'd departed the track. They stayed in touch by text message during the day, and every night that they were apart—too many, by Sarah's estimation—they talked until they were too sleepy to make sense. The topic didn't matter, only the feeling that they were drawing closer.

"You know what I mean," she said to Martin.

"Sadly, I'm afraid I do. You're in the high-school-crush phase of your relationship."

She laughed; Martin had her pegged.

"Exactly."

He sighed. "I'd rather see this happening with anyone but him."

"He's not in a league with Satan, you know."

"Satan is often in the eyes of the beholder."

She'd swap him her last baby potato for a little less Martin-drama.

"I don't expect Steve to become one of your best friends overnight," she said. "But I'm hoping you'll remember that *I* am. And I'm hoping you'll change your opinion of him, because I don't think you're being fair." She took a breath and said aloud the truth that grew daily. "I'm falling in love with him. In fact, I'm pretty much all the way there."

Martin's response was instantaneous. "You have to be joking."

"Actually, no, I don't. I know this probably seems strange from the outside, but—"

"*Strange?* It seems like utter madness, Sarah. You're an academic and he peddles wine now that he's through being a race car driver. Name one bloody thing that you have in common."

"Independence. Honor. Curiosity," she replied from the top of her head. "A love of wine. Driving fast. Midnight snacks."

Martin held up his hand. "Stop! Enough before I drown in syrup!" He shook his head. "I'll admit that you fancy yourself in love. The question is, does he fancy you back?"

"I think he does," Sarah said.

"Marvelous…for now."

"Thanks for the optimism."

"I simply don't want to see you get hurt."

"And I'm tired of being afraid of being hurt. Yes, it's a risk, but *you* hurt me, Martin, and yet I survived. We both did."

He fell silent for a moment, seemingly occupied by twirling the stem of his wineglass between his fingers.

"I don't suppose there's any real way one can talk a friend out of being in love, is there?" he asked.

"Doubtful."

"Then shall we talk logistics?"

She sighed. "If we must."

"So today, your beau is in, where?"

"Chicago. There's a race tomorrow and a winery event tonight."

"And you're here because…"

"I had a department meeting regarding curriculum, as you know."

"And that meeting was on top of your weekly Monday meetings. This is July, Sarah. You're not even teaching yet. What happens then?"

She took a sip of her wine. "A lot of weekend travel?"

"Seriously."

"I am serious. And I get it, Martin. I really do. There are countless reasons to set aside this whole relationship, but there's one reason I can't—love."

"And how does he feel about your plans for a child?"

Ouch. He would bring up the large pink-and-baby-blue elephant in the room. "I've never mentioned it."

"You say you're in love with this man and nearly drown me in the sweet reasons why, yet you've never mentioned to him something as life-altering as the fact that you've been planning to have a baby? You still do, don't you?"

"Of course I do. The topic just hasn't come up."

"I rather doubt that it would unless you raise it. You're beyond the standard nesting age, you know."

"Thanks for mentioning it."

He smiled. "Anytime, love. And you may feel free to tell me to keep my nose out of your love life, if you so wish."

Sarah began to feel as though they just might survive this messy conversation.

"You're my best friend, Martin…weird as that is. Of course I'm not going to tell you to butt out. And I know I probably should have mentioned something this fundamental to Steve, but the timing hasn't been good. It's just not a phone topic, and when we're together, I'm working to keep those times light."

"Romantic, but hardly a test of this love of yours."

"Can't I just be in love for a little while?"

"It's only love if you communicate."

She struggled to come up with something to refute that, but Martin had her pinned.

"Beast," she said.

He laughed. "I will take that in the very best way possible."

Just as she planned to take his relationship coaching.

NIGHT HAD FALLEN LONG AGO, and Sarah lay curled up under the covers, frequently waking from a restless sleep. Her cat lobbying to take up residence on her pillow wasn't helping matters.

"You're pushing it, Howard," she said.

Howard didn't have one heck of a lot to say in return. Usually, she was okay with the silent treatment, but tonight she needed a friendly voice.

She had known that Steve was going to be busy with the Pebble Valley gathering until after ten. Between that and the hour's time difference between Charlotte and Chicago, she hadn't really expected to hear from him before midnight. But now it was nearly two in the morning, and he'd neither called nor texted. She missed him.

Sarah rolled onto her side and retrieved her cell phone from the nightstand, literally taking matters into her own hands. With the push of one simple number, she was connected to Steve's phone. Even if he didn't answer, she would at least get his recorded message and leave one of her own.

"Hello?" said a deep voice over some sort of surrounding din.

"Hey," she replied loudly enough that Howard immediately shot to the foot of the bed. "How are you?"

"Tired, bored, missing you, but at least hearing some of the best blues music I have in a long time," Steve replied.

"Where are you?"

"Just dealing with business stuff," he said. "Are you okay?"

"I just wanted to hear your voice." Which she could…barely.

"Hang on. Let me see if I can find a quieter place."

Sarah felt like a voyeur, hearing muffled laughter, louder yet indistinct conversations, and then, finally, Steve again.

"The band is starting up," he said. "This isn't going to work."

"It's okay," she said.

"What?"

"I said, it's okay."

"Look, Sarah, I can't hear a damn thing now. I'll talk to you tomorrow. And I'll see you in Sonoma next Friday, right?"

NASCAR's mid-July break was approaching. Steve

was having a bash at the vineyard, and had asked her to come out and be with him. She'd be flying out with Dean and Patsy.

"Yes."

And if she and Steve had a few private moments, maybe they could really talk.

"All right. Gotta go. It's crazy here."

And then he was gone.

"Love you," Sarah said to no one at all.

CHAPTER ELEVEN

HOME.

Just as it had last time, that feeling of déjà vu, or whatever it was, swept over Sarah as she and the Grossos pulled up to Steve's house. She wondered now if it had been so much the house calling to her as its owner. Maybe that was what she had felt...what she continued to feel on top of a racing pulse and the sort of excitement that put her squarely in Martin's high-school-crush category.

Dean had barely gotten the car into Park before Sarah was out her door. She'd waited too many days to see Steve for patience to remain among her particular virtues.

The door to the house swung open but it wasn't Steve waiting to greet her. Instead, a tall and slender woman— probably somewhere in her late thirties—stood framed in the doorway.

"You must be Sarah," she said as Sarah approached. "You're exactly as Steve described. I'm Rosita, his housekeeper."

"It's nice to meet you, Rosita." She shook the woman's hand. "Steve talks about me?"

Rosita laughed, and the sound was as pretty as she. "Only all the time. I'm glad you're finally here."

"And I'm happier than you'll ever know."

"I'm sure you are. Steve's on a conference call in the den. He wanted me to bring you to him as soon as you arrived."

Sarah glanced back over her shoulder. Dean and Patsy were now out of the car, too, and smiling, no doubt over her impatience.

"I should get my luggage," she said.

"No need," Rosita said. "I'll see that it's handled."

"You're sure?"

"Positive." She smiled at the Grossos. "Welcome," she said. "You have two choices. You can stay in either the smaller guest suite here, as Mattie is in one of the larger ones and Steve's new business partner in the other. Or you can use the guesthouse."

"We'll take the guesthouse," Patsy replied for the couple. "I can do some shopping that way."

Confused, Sarah looked around. "There's a guest-house on the property? And shopping?"

"No, the guesthouse is actually a town house on the main square in Sonoma, where Steve lived before buying this place. He held onto it and uses it for overflow guests. Some of my favorite shops are just down the street. Maybe you'd like to stay there, too?" she asked teasingly.

Sarah laughed. "Tempting, but no."

"In that case, if you'll follow me…" Rosita said, one hand extended toward the open front door.

Patsy gave Sarah a quick hug and whispered, "Dean

and I are going to head to town. Take advantage of the privacy while you can."

Sarah had seen little of the inside of Steve's house the last time she'd been here. Now, though she really wanted to take in the details, she was too distracted by the thought of seeing Steve. As she followed Rosita, she did notice the rough and creamy interior stucco walls and the dark orange Mexican tile beneath her feet. Some of the tiles with a paw print or what looked to be chicken claw-prints in the surface. She smiled at the bits of whimsy in the otherwise austere architecture.

Rosita stopped at a closed door and knocked on the dark-stained wood. It swung open and Steve was there. He'd rolled up the sleeves to his light blue button-down shirt so that his forearms were exposed. His jeans were worn and snug, and his boots looked as though he'd walked the vineyard in them many, many times. He looked every inch a winemaker and every inch the man she'd missed so much over the past dozen days.

"Thank you," he mouthed to Rosita, and then ushered Sarah inside and closed the door again. She watched as he returned to his desk and hit a button on the speakerphone.

"It's now a one-way call," he said to Sarah as he approached her. "About time you're here. I've been thinking about you. A lot."

"Really? What have you been thinking?" She was asking for the fun of it. His slow and sexy smile had already led her in the direction of his thoughts.

"All manner of things," he said. "And in great detail."

She inclined her head toward the speakerphone, from

which a group of people seemed to be dryly discussing percentages and splits and defaults. "Your friends, won't they miss you if you're gone too long?"

"They won't miss me at all. It's just lawyers negotiating...the white noise of business."

"In that case..." She wound her arms around his neck and kissed him with the hunger she'd been hoarding all week.

Steve kissed her back even more thoroughly, then held her so tightly that she let out a little squeak when she tried to breathe.

"Sorry," he said. "I guess I really missed you."

"It's okay. Don't let go."

She tipped back her head as he ran a series of kisses down her neck.

"It would be rude of me to lock the door and not say hi to Dean and Patsy, wouldn't it?" he murmured against her skin.

It didn't seem to Sarah that he was looking for much in the way of guidance, since already he was toying with the hem to her top.

"Good news," she whispered. "They decided to head straight to the guesthouse."

"Good news, for sure," he replied.

Without letting go of her, he walked them both back to the door, and locked it.

In his arms, she was most definitely home.

When something was right, Steve believed in running with it. Problem was, he didn't know exactly where to run with Sarah. Out of his house would be the first option. He stood a better chance of having a quiet, private day with her down in the winery tasting room than he did in his own kitchen.

When he'd planned this party, he'd known this was the way it would be, but it had sounded more peaceful while off in the hazy future than when living it. The afternoon cookout was hours away, but the party rental people were already setting up, and soon guests with whom he needed a little extra face time would be arriving.

Rosita stood at the double wall oven, checking to see if her breakfast casserole was ready to be served. Mattie hovered over the coffeemaker, so impatient Steve was sure that any time now she'd pull out the pot of brew currently filling and stick her mug under the stream of coffee.

She glanced over at him, and he said, "Don't even think of it."

Sarah looked up from the newspaper she'd spread across the counter and was reading. "Don't even think of what?"

"Coffee thieving. I was talking to Mattie," he said in clarification.

Sarah nodded absently and turned back to the business section.

Over at the kitchen table, Dean and Patsy were flipping a coin to see if their day would be filled with Patsy's desired spa day or Dean's trail ride.

"Heads again," Patsy said. "Third time in a row, which I think has to mean something."

"Your coin is loaded?" Dean suggested.

"No, it means that we're having the couples' massage at the spa in Calistoga. I promise I won't make you try the mud bath, though."

Dean flipped the coin again, then muttered under his breath. It must have been heads again.

"Finally!" Mattie exclaimed from over at the coffee-maker. She poured herself a mug and then was about to open the refrigerator to peer inside when Rosita cleared her throat.

"Do you think anyone else might want coffee?" she asked while giving Mattie a pointed look. Steve tried not to grin as Mattie obediently took the coffeepot and began to offer it around. He wished he could pull the same trick with his kid.

Folding the newspaper section closed, Sarah thanked Mattie for her refill.

"You're welcome. Totally, in fact. I can't tell you how cool it is to see my dad dating someone your age."

"My age," she echoed, sounding a little bemused.

"You know, someone from his own generation?"

Sarah laughed. "Thank you."

"Ew. That didn't come out right," she said as she returned the pot to its warmer. "I probably shouldn't talk until I've had my third coffee. I mean, it's obvious that you're younger than Dad. He's past fifty, after all."

Steve had to laugh at that one. "By a few months, kid. But we get the picture. There's dirt in the vineyard younger than I am."

"Okay, so that came out totally wrong, too."

"It's tough to believe you work with words for a living," he said.

"That's different. I get to play with those on the page before I submit them."

"Maybe a little self-editing before you speak, then?" Steve suggested.

Mattie gave him a kiss on the cheek. "Good point. And now, before I make a bigger fool of myself, I think I'll go sit outside and let the caffeine work its way to my brain." And with that, she hightailed it outside.

"Sorry," Steve said to Sarah.

"Don't be. She's welcoming and sweet, and I didn't mind a bit. I know I'm forty-two, after all."

Steve shook his head in mock sorrow. "That old, eh?"

"Eight years younger than you, my friend," she said, then gave him a sunny smile. "And I have no intention of catching up."

Dean laughed. "You tell him, Sarah."

"Someone has to keep that humility in place when Mattie's not around," Sarah agreed.

"Good morning," Damon Tieri said as he entered the kitchen.

Steve hadn't realized Damon had already arrived. He must have gotten in late the prior night. They were officially partners now; the lawyers had the deal on paper. Not that Damon and he had let the lack of paper stop them prior to that. And, as he'd assured Damon, their paths had hardly crossed.

"Damon, I'd like you to meet Sarah, my girlfriend," Steve said.

Sarah laughed. "Girlfriend sounds weird." She walked over to Damon and held out her hand. "I'm Sarah Stanton, a friend of Steve's." She shot a smile Steve's way. "Could we just stick with that?"

Damon shook her hand, and Steve watched as they exchanged a brief greeting. Okay, so the girlfriend tag was a little strange, but he wanted some way to let the world know there was a connection between them…one that he felt more strongly every time he saw her.

Steve then introduced Damon to Dean and Patsy, though he'd already told Damon much about the Grossos, and vice versa.

"Do you mind if we talk business for a moment?" Damon asked the couple. "I know that technically, this a vacation for you."

"No problem at all," Dean said, wearing an "if it saves me from the spa" sort of smile. "Have a seat."

"I thought we'd talk a little about Steve's and my change in marketing focus for Pebble Valley," Damon said as he pulled out a chair at the kitchen table and sat.

Steve moved closer, so that he was standing beside Sarah at the counter, but didn't sit and join the group. He knew the direction in which Damon was heading; they'd discussed it earlier in the week, and Steve was all for it. He also knew that he could leave this in Damon's hands and not feel compelled to control every detail.

Easier said than done, of course. Having Sarah as a distraction was helping right now, but he couldn't always have her at his side. Learning to cede a little control would be a slow process.

"Steve and I have been talking about a broader marketing plan for Pebble Valley that involves NASCAR," Damon said. "Steve has done a great job of using NASCAR events as a springboard to introduce Pebble Valley wines, and it's time to take it to the next level. We're seeking a NASCAR driver for a Pebble Valley sponsor, but it has to be the right one. We need an up-and-comer, and someone who would also translate to more wine sales outside the NASCAR fan segment, too."

"I think that sounds like a wonderful idea," Patsy said. "I don't believe there's another sponsoring winery out there. This has good novelty appeal, too."

Damon nodded. "Exactly. And because no good idea goes undone forever, we're moving quickly. Kent is someone we're considering, as he's an extremely viable choice for Pebble Valley, if probably a little pricey. Among NASCAR Nationwide Series drivers we're looking at Kyle Jordan." He paused for an instant and smiled. "Shelly Green actually showed up here to make her pitch while you were at Daytona, but I'm not sure she's got all the ingredients we're looking for. This is a one-shot deal to get it right."

"I like his mind," Sarah whispered to Steve. "He's sharp."

He nodded.

"I'd also appreciate input from both of you, should you think of anyone else," Damon said to Dean and Patsy. "Steve has given me some ideas, and I've been doing my research, but I'm a believer in casting a wide net."

"We'll do some thinking on it," Dean replied. "Probably all the time I'm captive on the massage table. Patsy's hijacking me for the day."

Patsy laughed. "Want to try one more flip of the coin?"

"No. I know when fate has it in for me," Dean said. "It's a spa day."

Damon pushed back from the table. "Well, thank you both for agreeing to share your thoughts."

"We know that Steve and Pebble Valley are going to be big names in wine," Dean replied. "You did the right thing in joining the team."

Damon smiled. "No doubt about it. Winners win."

The doorbell rang, and as she exited the room, Rosita said, "No one leaves without breakfast."

"I think we're being held hostage by a casserole," Sarah murmured to Steve.

Rosita returned with Nathan Cargill and his girl-friend, Stacy Evans. Since Nathan was wrapping up a season covering as Dean's team manager, and Stacy was Kent's pit crew's strength and conditioning coach, no introductions were necessary with the Grossos. In fact, Patsy rose and gave both of them hugs.

Steve knew that Patsy had felt particular empathy for the hard time Nathan had been given by the press after the murder of his father, Alan Cargill, from whom she and Dean had bought Cargill-Grosso Racing. Nathan had been cleared of the murder but that hadn't been covered in the same detail as when he'd been under suspicion. Not juicy enough, Steve guessed.

Once the Grossos had taken a moment to greet Nathan

and Stacy, Steve did the introduction honors with Sarah. Then he moved on to Damon, even though Damon had already spoken to Nathan on a conference call regarding the division of power at Pebble Valley. In addition to Nathan's temporary duties for the Grossos, he also ran a well-respected management consultancy business. Steve had retained him to look over the Pebble Valley deal on his behalf since Damon had a stronger business background than he. Steve wanted workable equality, and it was worth a consultant's fees to be sure he had it.

In fact, he liked Nathan's approach so much that he'd asked him to come out to the vineyard early and have a long-term planning talk with Damon and him. He planned to ask Damon if Sarah could be in on the conversation, too. In the quiet conversations they'd had about business, her insights had wowed him...yet another reason he was finding their frequent separations tough. Her mind was as sexy as her body.

"Now that we're all here...everyone outside," Rosita announced. "My casserole and fresh-squeezed orange juice will taste best in the sunshine."

"I'm going to give Rosita a hand. I'll be out in a minute," Sarah said to Steve from over her shoulder. "Of course you could always stay and help, too."

She stood on tiptoe getting a stack of plates down from a cupboard shelf. As he took in the sleek curves of her form and her laughter as she and Rosita traded joking comments, he thought about Damon's comment—winners win. He'd make damn sure that held true with Sarah, too.

SARAH KNEW THAT SHE SHOULD feel replete, and from more than just from the wonderful breakfast Rosita had made. As she looked at this group gathered under the Sonoma sun, she marveled at how much richer her life had become. To think that knowing all of these people had led from one career choice—to find flexibility enough to welcome a baby into her life—was simply astounding.

A baby… Sometimes it seemed that she was wishing for too much. Perhaps she should be content with the wealth of friends and love that grew daily around her.

But a baby… She wanted one very much, and Steve needed to know this. She wouldn't be asking him to be the father, just to accept that while right now it was just Sarah, she had every hope of it being Sarah plus baby one day. And if he couldn't embrace that, she would give back all of this.

It was an unsettling thought, one that had kept her silent on the subject when she and Steve had been alone last night. That, and the fact that she'd been more deeply tired than she'd expected. A hectic cross-country lifestyle might work well for Steve, but it was taking a decided physical toll on her.

Still, whether or not she was ready, and whether or not she had the energy, Martin was right. Although on the normal scale of relationship development, it would be premature to mention baby plans to Steve, she had to. Their pace was too fast, too intense, too intimate, not to. Except clearly not today. If the massive party tent on the stretch of level land behind the house hadn't been hint enough, while Sarah had been in the kitchen, Rosita had been talking of guests in the hundreds. Sarah hoped some exaggeration had been involved.

Dean and Patsy, who, along with Damon, had just left, were flying out tomorrow. Sarah knew one thing for sure; she didn't want to go. She needed to be here longer, both to spend some time with Steve and to give herself a chance to recuperate. She expected to be in even greater need of a break after that party. She settled her hand on Steve's arm and leaned toward him.

"What do you think of me staying a few days longer?" she asked.

"Really? I thought you said you have a department meeting on Monday morning?"

"I'm pretty sure I can teleconference in. We even have people do it by Web cam when they're on leave."

His smile was broad and instantaneous. "I'm not set up for a Web cam, but if it will keep you here a while, I'll be by Monday morning."

A man of action. She had to like that, even if she wasn't quite sure she could keep up.

"Deal," she said.

He reached over and squeezed her hand. That small gesture of intimacy brought more warmth than the sunshine from above. Feeling more settled, Sarah turned her attention to the guests.

Mattie had jumped into conversation with Nathan Cargill. She wore the inquisitive expression that Sarah often saw on Steve's face.

"So, Nathan, if you don't mind my asking, is there

anything new in your father's murder case?" Mattie asked.

Steve shook his head. "Mattie, do you think you could at least wait until after lunch before starting an inquisition?"

"Sorry. Questions run in my blood."

"They definitely did when you where a child," Steve said.

Mattie smiled her agreement.

"I lived in terror of what she'd ask and where she'd do it," he added to Sarah.

Mattie laughed. "Jeez. A girl asks about the birds and the bees in the middle of the night just once and she's never forgiven."

"I wasn't alone," Steve said to Sarah. "Suffice to say that particular new romance went down in flames. As did the thought of ever making any more little girls."

"Ha! As if I'd slow you down," Mattie said.

He swept a glance around. "See any more Clayton progeny hanging around? No. Issue closed, and for good."

Sarah tried to ignore the knife-like cut to her confidence. Steve couldn't know how his words affected her. Not yet, anyway. She focused on the conversation instead of her own worries. Those could wait.

"If you don't want to talk about it, Nathan, I understand," Mattie was saying. "But your dad was always one of my favorite people. When I'd be at a race as a teenager, he'd always pay attention to me. Except for him, Dean and Patsy, I was invisible to the other adults. You were lucky to have him for a dad."

"I was, and I wish I'd spent more time with him back then, but you know how it goes…."

"Yup. Parents are always cooler when viewed through another kid's eyes. Right, Dad?"

Steve laughed. "According to you, I was the meanest dad ever."

"See what I mean?" Mattie asked Nathan. "But, really, I don't want to open up anything tough for you. I know that the past months can't have been easy."

"Life has a way of working itself back around," Nathan said, giving his girlfriend a look of such complete love that Sarah felt a little wistful. And Stacy was giving it right back to Nathan, too.

It must be nice to have the stars align, Sarah thought.

"I'm fine with talking about my dad," Nathan said to Mattie. "Especially to you."

"Thank you," she replied.

"A couple of days ago I got a call from the detective on the case, Lucas Haines. Know him?"

She shook her head. "I know the name, but haven't met him."

"He's around the tracks, so you're bound to run into him. In any case, they've apparently made an arrest…a man named Armando Mueller," Nathan said. "He's your basic street person…no job, no known address. They believe he came in and killed my father for whatever cash and pawnable goods he had on him…probably drug-related."

"Wow, so they think that a vagrant just walked in off the street and took the elevator to the ballroom area without being noticed as a little out of place in one of New York City's fanciest hotels? Interesting theory," Mattie said, her voice thick with doubt.

"Haines isn't exactly in love with the theory, either, but the guy confessed."

"Sure. It gets him off the street and into a place with cots and food for a while," said Steve, who had been listening intently.

Nathan nodded. "The same response I had. And Haines, too, but the powers that be are pushing it down on him. I think he's trying to push back, but..." He shrugged. "What I know is only as much as Haines chooses to tell me. And of course, since they were targeting me when I clearly had nothing to do with my dad's death, let's just say that I have a heightened level of skepticism."

"Understandable," Mattie said. "I've been following what news I could find on the case. After hearing this, I think I should look in to it a little more. I'm sure there's a story in this."

"And some publicity just might be the push that Haines's superiors need to get the case back on track," Nathan said. "Any help you can give would be appreciated."

"Anything. I adored your dad."

Nathan smiled. "Thank you for that."

Sarah felt Steve's hand again settle over hers. She glanced over at him, and her heart turned a loop at the warm look in his eyes. Some of the wistfulness she'd been feeling drifted off. Maybe their stars hadn't aligned, but she so wanted them to.

CHAPTER TWELVE

THE DIFFICULTY WITH A 9:00 a.m. faculty meeting in North Carolina was that it translated to 6:00 a.m. in Sonoma. Sarah had slipped from bed, dressed California casual and headed to the den for her meeting via Web cam. Now, a full hour and more later, she remained captive in front of the computer, updating her fellow faculty on the current confirmed list of new internship opportunities, as well as discussing the possibility of student recruitment at NASCAR races.

While she appreciated the technology helping her to be present while a continent away, she knew she was missing the nuances of what was happening in that room. And what she thought she was catching, she was none too comfortable with. Even Alden, her staunchest supporter, had grumped a bit at her form of attendance. And more than once, meeting members had raised a question, only to then conclude that the matter would be more easily dealt with in person. On some level, Sarah had to agree. Still, she expected that with a little more sleep and a little more energy, she'd be feeling more receptive, too. Adding to her distraction was her phone, which she'd set on vibrate only, buzzing with the arrival of new text messages.

When the meeting agenda rolled on to topics she wouldn't have to speak about, Sarah surreptitiously slid the phone toward her, then brought it to her lap so she could scroll through the messages. The first was from Steve, telling her that the bed seemed empty without her. She ducked her head to hide her wide smile from the Web cam and then checked out the next message. Where are you? Martin had sent.

Sarah hit reply and let him know that she was still in California. A few moments later a message came back.

So no call to tell me?

She shook off a slight feeling of irritation. While she had no reason to share her daily whereabouts with Martin, they'd both done it for so many years that she supposed he might feel a little miffed.

Sorry. It was a last-second decision. A fib, she knew, but she didn't want pressure or a lecture from him.

I need you to look at a new grant application.

Sarah relaxed. There was no lecture in store, just a quick review of his work, which was something they also frequently did for each other. Bringing grant money into the college shortened the road to tenure, and competition for foundation and government grants was fierce, so every word in an application had to be honed to its optimal effect.

E-mail it. Will get back to you asap, she wrote.

"Sarah?"

She looked up at the sound of her name floating from the computer's speakers.

"Yes?"

"I was asking if you'll be back in town for the meeting next week?"

Would she? For a moment, she imagined staying here until she joined the Grossos for the Indianapolis race, then coming back to Sonoma with Steve. She needed to give this bicoastal routine a try, but she also needed to make her job work.

"Yes…. At least, right now I'm planning to," she said to her boss.

"Either way. It wouldn't hurt to give the Web meeting format another try. Right now, I'm somewhat underwhelmed."

"I know we can make this work," she replied with more vigor than she actually felt. Unless they moved the department meetings to Tuesdays, to suit her Tuesday through Thursday teaching schedule, this was as optimal a situation as she could wish for. "One way or another, I'll see you all next Monday."

After she'd signed out of the meeting, Sarah logged onto the college's server to check her work mail. There were the usual e-mails from past students looking for letters of recommendation, college administration updates and a sprinkling of more personal correspondence. Last was the e-mail from Martin, with a document attached.

The e-mail's body read only "fyi," so she clicked on the attachment to check out the body of his proposal. It was only then that she noticed the file she was downloading was in a photo format. Sarah watched as the picture slowly began to reveal itself, wondering if Martin had overnight morphed into one of those people who sent photos of kittens or puppies or whatever with cute little captions added.

Apparently not.

Chicklets seemed within his realm of interests, though.

In the photo, Steve stood in some party venue with a wineglass in his right hand and his left arm draped around the standard model of underdressed and overendowed female. She was looking up at him adoringly, and he was giving her the same slow smile Sarah had warmed under so many times over the past several weeks.

Sarah minimized the image, reminding herself that there were countless photos like this floating around the Internet, and that if Martin had decided to do a little digging of his own, so be it. She needed to desensitize herself to these old pictures if she planned to be with Steve. He'd told her he wanted to change the way he used his time for marketing; these were his past, not his present.

She brought the image back up on the screen, and this time she noted something more. There was a second page to the document. In this photo, the young woman sat on Steve's lap and appeared to be laughing at something he said. Behind Steve and the chicklet was a low stage with two musicians, and behind them was a neon sign in sloped script that read Blue Note. Last week, when he'd been in Chicago, Steve has said something about blues music.

So what? Sarah thought, but went to her trusty search engine nonetheless. She typed in a query limiting results to items posted in the past two weeks. Steve and the chicklet in question popped right up. Before she could talk herself out of it, Sarah opened the window and hit the print button.

Her desire for a child and stability, his chosen life-style, their cross-country locations—all of this mattered. Much as she wanted to live a full-time fantasy, she needed honesty and communication from Steve. She needed his support, not another reason to doubt herself and this entire situation when she already felt pretty damned drained. Sarah reached for the printer, pulled the photo and went in search of its subject.

WHY WAS IT THAT MONDAY HAD a way of sneaking up on a guy?

Steve stood in the kitchen trying for thirty seconds of his own in which to chug a glass of orange juice and maybe get a piece of toast started. His lawyer was on the cell phone talking about some new endorsement deal, Rosita was waving the land line's handset at him and Kyle sat at the kitchen table watching the show.

He turned his back on everyone but the lawyer going on in his ear and finished that call. When he turned back, Sarah had appeared. She looked gorgeous, with her hair loose and her jeans and white scoop-necked shirt fitting perfectly. She had a piece of paper in her hand; despite the fact that he had back-to-back meetings all day, he hoped it was a reservation for a quiet room at one of the local inns. He smiled at her, but she didn't give him one in return.

Not good.

Steve pocketed his cell phone, requested that Rosita take a message, and asked Kyle if he could meet up with him in just a couple of minutes. Once he'd cleared the kitchen of all but Sarah, he came over intending to kiss her full on the mouth, but got a quick turn-of-face move so that his kiss became more a brotherly brush against her cheek.

Not good at all.

"What's wrong?" he asked.

She presented him with a photo printed on a piece of copy paper. It didn't take more than a second for him to recognize it as one taken in Chicago, the week before. He wouldn't call it incriminating so much as it had been awkward. The girl had sat herself down, uninvited. He'd ushered her to her feet a moment later and agreed to a couple more photos with her before sending her on her way. Once Sarah knew this, she'd see the picture as nothing more than what it was…a minor irritant.

Just then, his cell phone rang.

"Was this last weekend?" Sarah asked over the music of the ring tone.

"Yes." He pulled out the phone and looked at the caller identification. It was his lawyer again.

He waggled the phone. "I really have to—"

"I'd like to talk about this without interruption," she said.

Steve let the call go to voice mail, but Sarah didn't look any happier.

This was what he got for not listening to instinct. Instinct had told him that he should have brought up his night in Chicago. He had semilistened to that voice, but *later* had always seemed a better time, and now it was too late.

She gestured at the photo. "You two look as though you know each other pretty well."

He couldn't quite peg the muted light in her eyes. It wasn't anger, but it spoke of something that didn't bode well for him.

"We've met a couple of times," he said. "Don't make this out to be more than it is."

"And how am I making it out to be?" Her voice remained calm, but something was just flat-out *off*.

"You're making it into a big deal when it's just part of the game and something I can't change. If I were involved with every woman who's had her picture taken with me, I would have died of exhaustion before hitting thirty."

"That's not funny."

His phone rang again. Lawyers were a persistent breed, and this one had a deal hanging in the balance, which was going to make the guy relentless.

"Look, I need to take this call or they're never going to leave me alone. Why don't we meet in the den and really talk about this in a few minutes?" Steve asked, then looked at his watch. "Damn. I've got two accountants and one of Damon's people here in five minutes. I'm sorry. This is one helluva morning for me."

She nodded briskly. "It's business. I understand."

"Okay, right before lunch, then?"

Her smile was brief and didn't quite make it to her eyes, but Steve figured that was the best he was going to get in the time available. Sarah left the kitchen, and Steve returned his lawyer's call.

As SARAH GAZED OUT THE WINDOW of the hired car, she pretended she was a tourist. In a way, she had been just that. Over the past weeks, she'd been visiting another land, another life. One that was never meant to be hers. That sense of home while at Pebble Valley was just as illusory as the little game that she'd played with herself. She had pretended that she could have it all—job, child, excitement, lover…each element at no cost to the rest of her life. And she might have, too, had the lover been willing to balance all of these crazy elements, too. But she saw now how busy he was, and how set in his ways. Communicating with her was a sacrifice when it would have needed to have been a priority.

Ahead of her, the peaks of the Golden Gate Bridge appeared. Though the sun still shone, fog had begun to curl down the craggy cliff sides to the bay. She knew that the chill air of San Francisco awaited, just as the chill of reality had settled into her bones.

Despite this recent foray into sheer feeling, she remained a logical woman. Being slighted over the chicklet was natural, though overemotional. It had been one photograph, one split second in time. Sarah knew to her core that nothing had happened between Steve and the girl. He believed in sexual fidelity, if not particularly marriage, and she was okay with that. The chicklet hadn't been what had driven her to call a driver and get herself put on standby for a flight home.

It's all just part of the game....

Those words had been a jolt back to reality.

What would never be okay was his lack of real interest in changing his external playboy persona. He'd shrugged it off so cavalierly. Steve Clayton could not be the man she needed in her—and perhaps one day, her child's—life. Oh, he'd said all the right things those nights when he'd held her in his arms...speaking of a slower lifestyle, one in which he could be home on his land, growing a new life that blended all that he loved. She had been able to see herself in that image, but not the one with the smug, grinning man.

Sarah's car had taken the bridge's outside lane, and she watched the tourists snapping photos and walking the span's broad pedestrian expanse. The morning traffic slowed, then stopped. Outside her window, against the bridge's thick rail, a couple stood hand-in-hand, the guy speaking earnestly. When he was done, the girl nodded excitedly, and then they kissed, the other tourists continuing past them in a stream. Sarah turned away. It was too much to see that intimacy and love.

Steve had always made love to her with a caring that had gone deeper than passion. That hadn't been an act, she was certain. And maybe he really wanted to change, much as she wanted to start exercising more and eating better. Just not enough to actually do it.

The traffic picked up pace, and they made their way into the hilly and populous terrain of the city as they headed south, toward San Francisco International Airport. This was a beautiful place, eclectic and exciting…one she'd imagined sharing with Steve.

But until Steve elected otherwise, he would be the man with the broad grin and the young women. To him, it was simply part of the game, with no deeper meaning. Whether she could let their relationship move forward, knowing that she'd see those sorts of things virtually every time he was on a publicity junket, stood as a separate issue.

She'd been cheated on by not one, but two men she'd loved. That was her baggage and her fault that she'd spent too many years afterward avoiding intimacy. And it was her issue that she doubted her own strength to handle being with a man whose image and choices so conflicted with her personal needs.

Too much separated them: miles, lifestyles and freely chosen paths. She couldn't have it all, so she would choose to let go of Steve. And hope one day, she would find her heart again.

CHAPTER THIRTEEN

FOCUS.

The meeting going on in front of Steve was important, dammit. Documents, decisions and dollars flew around the room, all of which would affect him and his business for years to come. And yet he couldn't focus. He hadn't been able to since Sarah had walked out almost three weeks ago.

"Steve?" Damon asked.

"What?"

His partner gestured at the door to the attorneys' conference room. "Let's step out for a minute, shall we?"

Steve looked around the table at the faces looking back at him. He must have zoned out and missed another question. He rose.

"If you'll excuse us?" he said to the others in the room.

No one objected to his departure, likely because he'd already been mentally absent.

"Look," Damon said once they were out in the hallway, "I'm sure there are others who'd like to give you the same speech, and they don't even have as much on the line as I do right now. You need to get over this funk or whatever it is that you've been in and rejoin the world. You're going to end up costing us money if you keep on checking out."

Steve could have lied and said he didn't know what Damon was talking about, but the younger man was too smart to buy into that.

"You're right," he said. "And I'm working on it, okay?"

"Is this about Sarah?" Damon asked.

The question didn't surprise Steve on one level because he and Damon had reached the point where they discussed more than business, but it did surprise him that Damon would get this personal. Steve was slow in answering.

"Hey," Damon said. "It's not as though it takes a whole lot of perception to see what's going on. You've been like this since she left. I genuinely like you and I'm genuinely worried about you."

Steve looked down at the ground and used his right hand to ease some of the tension from the back of his neck. Even her name got to him.

"Yeah, it's Sarah."

"So fix it."

Right. Life should be so easy.

First, he'd shoved aside the B.S. note she'd left him about differing goals and tough logistics and how he should just let this end now, naturally and painlessly. He couldn't speak for her, but he was feeling plenty of pain and probably would until he knew what had really sent her on a crazy cross-country journey to avoid him.

After a handful of calls, Sarah had finally picked one

up. While she'd been polite, she'd been about as emotionally forthcoming as the concrete Venus in her living room. She'd had enough time to come up with her script and she was sticking to it.

For about a week after the phone call of ritual politeness, Steve had conducted a written campaign. He'd had notes delivered to her house with as many varieties of lavender plants as he could find without going to France and digging up the buggers, himself. Still she had maintained her silence.

Following that he'd lapsed into what he liked to think of as his introspective phase, which was more of an ego stroke than admitting the truth. He was in a serious funk over a woman who wanted nothing to do with him.

A woman whom he apparently loved…

But since he could say none of this to his partner, who was patiently dealing with him, he said only, "I've been working on a fix, but it doesn't look like it's going to happen."

Damon nodded. "Then at the risk of sounding callous, maybe you should get on with business?"

Business. It had been the one thing consistently there for Steve. Days ago he'd concluded that his land and the wine were his future. And now he was feeling just a little ticked off, too. When a guy came right down to it, Sarah Stanton was being a fool to throw away all of this. Hell, to throw away *him!* The time had come to grab hold of what he *did* have and make damn sure that Sarah saw that life rolled on just fine without her.

"You, my friend, are one hundred percent correct," Steve said. "Let's get back in there and kick some business butt."

WHAT DID ONE DO WITH THREE DOZEN lavender plants, once one's garden was full? And heaven knew that Sarah's garden was full. Avoiding the mid-August sun, she sat beneath the shade of the live oak tree that occupied the back corner of her yard. She looked at her home…her place of refuge. She needed it now, more than ever. Steve was back in full swing, with new pictures of him with fresh and perky chicklets popping up daily.

This quiet life was what she had wanted, though. She'd known him better than he'd known himself, and she'd been right to let this whole relationship wither, much as the last, unplanted lavender plants were currently doing. She wasn't letting them die because they were innocent messengers from Steve, but because she could hardly find the will to pull herself together for work, let alone handle any extras.

Her garden was complete, and she was pregnant.

There was some balance in that, she supposed. And no small amount of humor, either. The giver of the plants had given far more than either of them had expected.

Though she hadn't yet been to the doctor, the six positive pregnancy tests—and who had any idea there were so many varieties on the market?—couldn't all be wrong. Her own body had let her know, too. She'd been feeling slowed, sleepy and almost as though her body was paying attention to someone other than she. At first, she'd thought it was a sorrow bordering on depression over having left Steve. But then she'd realized that it must have been something different, and decidedly more.

Six pregnancy tests didn't lie, and she was elated. Not that she had the energy to act very elated. Food wasn't exactly tops on her list. Lounge chairs, naps and more naps were. Today, she'd made plans to meet up with Martin, then called him back to say that maybe another day might be better. He'd agreed readily enough, which was good, as she didn't have the energy on this sticky day to tell him that she was pregnant. She couldn't even broach the thought of telling her mother.

Sarah rose from the warm earth and slowly meandered back toward her house and the utter bliss of air-conditioning. The lavender plants could wait, as could everything else in her life. Right now, she wanted to focus on being Sarah...pregnant Sarah. She paused to breathe deep and do just that.

"No wonder you haven't been answering," Martin said as he rounded the side of her house. "I've been ringing the front bell for the past five minutes and was about to break in."

"Break in? Why?"

"No one's actually seen you in over a week, Sarah."

"Oh, for heaven's sake, you just talked to me on the phone this morning."

"And I didn't like what I heard," he said. "I'm hardly waiting for the 'Larchmont Professor Found Eaten by Cat' headline."

"I'm sure Howard would continue to prefer his dry food," she replied.

Martin laughed. "All right, then. We'll leave Howard out of this and get down to the fact that I'm worried about you. You haven't been in the office, you've missed all of the group's lunches, and you're not even answering your e-mail with any regularity. What sort of ex-husband would I be if I didn't come over to check on you?"

"The standard sort?"

Regardless, she opened the sliding door from the patio and ushered him inside. With Howard—and Martin—at her heels, she went to her favorite nesting spot, the sofa, and flopped out. Martin stood over her, no doubt trying to decide if she truly was approaching that dreaded "eaten by cat" state.

"I still have a pulse," she said to him. And apparently the moment had arrived to tell him what else she had humming along inside of her. She rolled onto her side and propped her head with a pillow, then waved her hand toward the armchair. "You might as well sit down. That hovering is going to exhaust me."

Martin sat, and Howard hopped onto the couch and curled up behind Sarah's knees.

"I know I've been a little low-profile since I came back from California, but I've had a lot to sort out, and I thought it would be best if I did it on my own."

"Long-distance relationships are difficult, Sarah. Don't beat yourself up over not being able to coordinate one."

She shook her head. "It wasn't the distance in miles so much as in life choices. Ours didn't mesh well. Add that to the logistics and you have…well, me on the couch feeling like hell."

"It will get better. I promise. After we split, I spent every evening for a month straight on my couch… which, I thank you for leaving me…along with a fifth of Irish whiskey."

"No whiskey for me, or wine, either," she said.

"Good choice."

"A necessary choice." She drew in a deep breath and said what she hadn't voiced aloud to anyone, not even her cat. "Martin, it seems that I'm pregnant."

"It *seems?*"

"Well, I'm not officially pregnant. I haven't been to a doctor, but I've tried those home pregnancy tests…a lot of them, actually."

He leaned back in his chair and observed her almost as if he'd never before seen her. "You're pregnant, then. I'd ask how this happened, but the answer is fairly apparent."

It felt good to talk about this. It had been too great a burden to carry alone. "To you, maybe, but not to me. We used protection every time, but obviously—"

Martin raised his hand. "Stop. I understand the process and would much rather not linger on the details."

She nodded. "Right. Of course."

"So, what's next?" he asked.

"Other than the obvious move of giving birth to this baby, I don't know," she admitted. "Really, I don't even want to think about it. I just want to revel a little in the fact that this is happening at all."

"And about the father?" Martin asked.

"I don't know," she said, repeating the phrase that ran

through her mind every single time she thought of Steve. "It's safe to say that he's picked up with his old life."

"If he ever left it at all."

"I like to think he did…at least a little bit."

Martin nodded. "I'm sorry. That was my anger speaking. I'd expect he did change. You're worth that and much more, Sarah."

Damn tears. Along with revulsion for nearly every food group, she'd also been dealing with tears that arrived both frequently and sometimes meaninglessly. But when it came to real things—like what Martin had just said— she was a certifiable mess. She wiped at her eyes.

"Should I get you a tissue or something?" he asked, sounding more uncomfortable than she felt.

"No…just give me a second to get it back under control."

"Fine," he said after clearing his throat.

"Here's the thing," Sarah said once she was sure that she'd shut down her tear ducts. "I never quite got around to that conversation with Steve about wanting a baby. I meant to, but the more I looked at the situation, the more I knew it would never work. He's set in his ways and has a life that doesn't have room for extra obligations. I think that this should be my issue, my child."

"And you don't plan to tell him?"

She pointed to the sofa's side table, where she'd left a stack of photos and clippings she'd printed. "Check those out."

Martin picked up the papers and began flipping through them. "He's a busy man."

"Yes, he is, and I'm not just talking about the girls you see. Steve's business is at the tipping point. If it's going to succeed on the level that he and his partner envision, the next couple of years will be among the busiest in his life, and that's saying a lot."

Martin set the papers down. "All of which leads up to?"

"This is my baby, my dream. It wouldn't be fair to dump all of this on Steve right now."

"I see," Martin replied.

She had expected a more vocal ally. "It's not as though I never plan to tell him. But why now? Believe me, I witnessed enough conversations that made it clear that he has no interest in getting back on the daddy track. I don't want him to think that I expect anything from him emotionally or financially. I can do this on my own. And in any case, the two of us have already fallen a little short on the emotional front or we'd still be together."

Martin sat silent for a moment. "So you don't plan to cut him out entirely?"

"No." But only because she felt a little squirmy even thinking of that.

With that, Martin seemed to relax. "Well, that's sensible, at least. Steve Clayton might not be among my favorite people, but I can hardly see letting him go on blithely through life not knowing he'd fathered a child."

Sarah nodded. "I agree, but I also want to start as I plan to continue."

He glanced at Steve's current events photos. "There's some reason in that, also."

"I need your support, Martin," she said. "I know that

this is a lot to dump on you, but you've been my best friend forever, and if you can't understand how I feel about this…I don't…"

Damned miserable tears! They washed through her with a sea of emotion: sorrow, excitement, fear and something that felt like grabby, nasty guilt. She drew a shaky breath. "Please, I don't want to be alone."

He left his chair, came to the sofa and settled her into his arms. "Just bloody cry, would you? You're not alone."

And so Sarah cried, but felt more alone than ever.

CHAPTER FOURTEEN

AUGUST IN MICHIGAN'S Irish Hills was nearly as perfect a place and time as anyone could want. Maybe anyone except Steve. He was in the midst of his standard pre-race gathering for Pebble Valley, surrounded by wine lovers, fans and even a few really attractive women. To an outsider, and to more than one of his friends, he looked to be at the top of his game.

How could one woman have worked her way so quickly and deeply into his life? He'd asked Patsy if Sarah would be at the race, but the answer was no...as it had been since the day she'd walked from Pebble Valley.

Dean nudged his elbow. "Good crowd."

"Best yet," Steve replied.

"So enjoy it."

"I am."

Dean's snort pretty much expressed his level of disbelief. "Save it for someone who will buy in. Or better yet, back down from the battle lines and call the woman."

"No can do," Steve replied.

"You mean *won't* do." Dean took a swallow of wine and shook his head. "I know you have your faults, buddy, but I never thought stupid was among them."

Steve looked for some sort of pithy response, but came up short. He'd been doing that a lot, lately. Hell, his life had been doing that.

"Do it," Dean said. "Before it's too late."

SARAH SET DOWN HER CUP OF ice chips and slowly edged from the sofa at the sound of her doorbell. Though it hadn't felt particularly good, she had risen since Martin's visit yesterday. At least, she'd been up long enough to go to bed, sleep, wake, feel ill, shower, then start the whole exciting cycle again.

When she swung open the door, she was greeted by the largest bunch of lavender roses she'd ever seen. From somewhere behind them, she heard Martin saying, "I trust you have a big enough vase?"

"I'm not sure if the urn on the front porch will hold all of that."

"Improvise," Martin said, handing the bundle over to her.

He followed her to the kitchen, where she pulled three vases from the cupboard and then looked for her garden shears to trim stems. Martin leaned against the counter, lazily watching her.

"Interesting wardrobe choice," he said.

She looked down at the tie-dyed cotton sundress she'd pulled from the back of a drawer. It had last been out during her college days, but it was soft and loose, two requirements to soothe her frazzled nerve endings.

"Functional and nostalgic," she said, then set to work on the roses while Martin showed some initiative and put water in the vases.

"They're beautiful," she said. "My favorites, and I can't recall ever having gotten a bunch this fragrant."

"Hormones," he said.

She smiled. "That's an upside, all right. It almost makes up for the fact that the only thing I can keep down is ice."

"According to the book I bought last night, matters will improve once you reach your second trimester."

"Which seems a lifetime away." She paused as the rest of what he'd said sunk in. "You bought a book?"

"It's not as though I have any personal experience in pregnancy," he replied.

When the flowers were settled, Martin took her by the hand and led her back to her sofa. Once she was seated, she expected him to do the same, but he just stood there, frowning down at her.

"This isn't quite how I'd imagined it," he said.

"Imagined what?"

He didn't answer the question, and instead went back to the kitchen. In two trips he had all the roses in the living room.

"Can't do much about the dress, but this is better," he said.

"What's better?"

He went down on one knee, and Sarah felt her stomach very unromantically rise. She sucked in a deep breath to calm herself.

"Sarah, I would very much like to marry you…
again."

"Martin…"

"No, let me finish this. It was my fault that our
marriage ended. I fed you a whole lot of rot about males
not being made to be monogamous and you saw
through it, as you should have. I was immature and
made a poor choice. But we're both older now, both
wiser, I think, and I don't want to see you alone. So,
please, marry me."

"You wouldn't be doing this if I weren't pregnant."

"Ah, but there you're wrong. I would. I've just never
found the right moment…the right reason…to ask you
to let me back into your life."

Sarah sought the right words. "You're in my life
more than any man ever has been. You're a good
man…a wonderful friend, but we don't love each other."

He shook his head. "This kneeling is hell on the knees."

Martin settled next to her and took both of her hands
in his. "But I do love you, Sarah. In fact, I'm in love with
you in every sense of the term."

She could hardly argue him out of love, any more
than he'd been able to argue her. "Martin, I love you as
the dear friend that you are, but I'm not in love with you.
Not in that way."

"It seems to me that love in 'that way' hasn't been
working out so well with you. Shall we try it our way
and build a life together?"

"This is truly the kindest thing anyone has ever done
for me, but no…I can't. You deserve someone who's

crazy in love with you. What I can do is be your very best friend, and you can be this baby's Uncle Martin, the cool uncle who spoils this child rotten and lets him or her get away with stuff that uncool Mom never will."

"You're not going to let me do this for you, then?"

"What? And have you resent me for as long as we both shall live? Tempting as it is to have the security and comfort of you around 24/7, no."

He sighed and leaned back against the couch. "I don't know what else to offer but my heart."

Her tears welled, and this time it wasn't just pregnancy hormones. "For that, I'm sorry. I wish I could make it better for you. Unrequited love is most definitely the pits."

He pulled her close and gave her a hug. "It is, isn't it, love?"

Damn tears. Sometimes they served their purpose.

ON TUESDAY AFTERNOON, SARAH ditched the tie-dyed sundress in favor of a scoop-necked top and a print silk skirt she'd picked up on her shopping orgy with Patsy, weeks ago. After a phone lecture from her friend for her disappearing act, Sarah knew that she had to see her or risk heightening Patsy's already keen instincts. And so here she was, about to enter an uptown café, which undoubtedly smelled of food, for a lunch which she would not keep down.

Steeling herself for the onslaught of culinary sights and scents that could send her over the edge, Sarah entered the restaurant. Patsy was ensconced in the corner booth, as befit a local celebrity. She gave a cheery wave to Sarah, who had pinned on a smile over gritted teeth, holding back nausea.

Once Sarah had neared, Patsy rose and gave her a warm hug.

"It's good to see you," she said. "We've missed you. *All* of us have."

Sarah only nodded at the thinly veiled reference to Steve. She was sure the man had made all the right noises about regretting her absence. She was equally sure that he'd long ago recovered from any real sense of loss. She slid into the booth and thanked heaven for the cool air-conditioning. Already she could feel her palms and upper lip growing a little sweaty as she fought back the advancing nausea.

"It's about time you stepped away from your desk and saw the light of day," Patsy said. "You're looking a little pale."

No shock. She was feeling a lot pale.

"It's good to have a minute to get away," she fibbed.

Patsy nodded. "I know the feeling. We've been busier than ever at the office. Since I got here a minute or two before you, I've taken a look at the menu."

Sarah flipped hers open out a sense of obligation. She already knew that she was asking for as benign a meal as she could think of: green salad, no dressing and ice water.

"Though I'm not usually one for burgers, I have to say that the turkey burger with portabella mushrooms and roasted peppers looks great," Patsy said.

Under the best of circumstances, Sarah found ground turkey suspect. Something in the coloring was just flat-out *off*. And right now even the thought of the meat was proving to be too much.

"Be right back," she said, then fled the booth for the door marked Ladies…her current home away from home.

A few minutes later, after she'd rinsed her mouth and washed her face with cool water, and was just summoning the strength to go deal with more trial by food, Patsy entered the bathroom.

"I thought maybe you'd slipped out the back way," she said cheerily. "If you don't like my taste in restaurants, there's always the Lebanese place down the street. Their lamb is to—"

She stopped short at Sarah's violent shake of her head. "I'll be darned," she said. "You're pregnant."

Sarah decided to take the clueless route. It wasn't her favorite, but she lacked the energy for deception.

"Pregnant?" she echoed.

Patsy gave an impatient sigh. "Don't bluff. You've heard the word before…with child…a bun in the proverbial oven—pick your term, but you're pregnant."

"Why would you possibly say that?"

"Because I know that look, and I recall all too well the way my stomach would turn at the sight of certain foods. You are pregnant, Sarah Stanton, and don't you dare deny it."

Another woman who'd just entered the bathroom paused as though she intended to join in on the analysis.

"Can we do this back at the table?" Sarah asked.

"Of course," Patsy replied. "So long as you're through trying to fool me."

"I am. There's no point."

"So, now, then," Patsy said when they returned and she'd had a glass of ice water delivered to Sarah. "Let's get the most important question out of the way. How are you feeling?"

"Sick," Sarah replied. "But this morning the doctor assured me that I'm doing well. So long as I can keep down at least some of my vitamins and weather the next few weeks, I'll be fine."

"It's tough, though, isn't it?" Patsy asked, sympathy softening her voice.

"Meat," Sarah said. "I can't stand it. I can smell it from the moment I enter a market or restaurant, and it's not a good thing."

"Oh, you'll eat meat again. Soon enough, you'll do nothing but eat. Promise."

Sarah allowed herself a quick glance at the food arrayed on a nearby table. "The vegetarian life is looking pretty good to me."

"And who is going to be in this vegetarian life?"

Sarah knew what Patsy was asking, but she preferred not to answer. "The usual suspects. I have classes to teach and a life to lead. I'm hoping you'll always be a part of that life, too."

"And the baby's father?"

"A donor," she replied. "No issue."

Patsy laughed, but there was little humor in her tone. "Liar. You're telling me that after you and Steve spent weeks mad for each other, barely able to be apart, that during that time the two of you didn't make love once, and that you got yourself to a fertility clinic?"

"Yes?" It might have worked better had she not delivered her response as a question.

"Nice try." Patsy pushed aside her iced tea. "Now, none of this is my business, since I doubt you had any plans to volunteer that you're pregnant, but the secret's out, and Steve is one of my dearest friends."

"This is difficult, Patsy. I'm not denying that."

"And have you thought about Steve?"

Sarah's laugh almost hurt. "Thought about him? Every day. I have feelings for him. I just don't know what I'm going to do about him."

"Do about him? I'm not so very sure this is your choice. He's the father. He helped make this baby, and he has the right to know."

"Not now. Not yet."

"You can't say that so firmly. You need to think about what this means." She hesitated, then said in a tight voice, "I know the pain of having lost a child."

Sarah's heart ached for her friend, but she couldn't back down. "I understand how you feel, but this child isn't lost, Patsy. My situation isn't yours."

She gave a rueful shake of her head. "Maybe, but I can guarantee it's going to feel that way to Steve."

"Why?"

"Because every day he doesn't know he's going to be a father is a day of excitement and involvement that you have robbed from him. He'll never get those back, Sarah. Never."

"You're anticipating that he'll care. He's not exactly father material."

Patsy answered after a pause. "Once, I might have agreed with you. But maybe, now, at this point in his life, he's perfect father material."

"That, I can't see. I read the news, and yes, I do check up on Steve. He's in the same mode he's been in his entire adult life...work hard and party harder."

"I told you before, and it's still true. He allows the world to see only what he wants it to."

"I think maybe the image has merged with his reality."

"You do because it suits your purposes."

Sarah was growing angry. "Which are?"

"To keep Steve away so that you don't have to hear that he doesn't want to be a part of this. But think, Sarah, what if he does? What if he misses you as much as you do him?"

"Not possible," she replied, then ducked her head since she didn't need to share her case of the weepies with the restaurant.

"Call him. Tell him," Patsy urged.

She wiped at one stray tear. "I can't. Not yet. And I'm begging you not to tell him. I know he's your friend, and I know that our history could never measure up to what you've had with him. But I need this. I *really* need this."

"You're asking a lot."

"I'm asking for the chance to breathe...to figure things out. I need to be strong in myself before I can deal with this. And I have to tell you that between the hormone surge and having one of my wildest wishes come true, I don't even know who I am."

Patsy smiled. "I recall the feeling. And when you do recall who you are…?"

"I'll tell him. I swear I will, Patsy."

Her friend shook her head. "I hope for everyone's sake, that's soon. Because, Sarah, I have to say that you're making a real mistake. Both of you are better than this."

CHAPTER FIFTEEN

LATE WEDNESDAY EVENING, a glass of his new red blend before him, Steve sat at the bar of his empty tasting room, looking around at the outward trappings of his hard work. He'd done well at pushing this place along and would do better with Damon on the team. This part of his life was good. As for the rest, well, he had no lack of company, at least.

He planned to take a breather tomorrow…a day when he'd do nothing more than shoot the breeze with his winemaker and maybe go visit some of his pals in the valley. Most of the small wineries held a monthly rotating picnic where they'd share ideas and marketing suggestions. Steve had missed the last few and he wanted to catch up.

His cell phone, sitting on the bar next to one damn stellar glass of wine, began its "answer me" song. He almost ignored it, except it could be Mattie, with whom he'd been playing a drawn-out game of phone tag. When he looked at the caller ID, though, it was Patsy. Patsy almost never called him. She just sent word through Dean, since they spoke pretty much daily.

"Hello?"

"Hi, Steve. I'm just calling to see how the heck you're doing."

Her voice was lyrical, almost sappy sugar sweet…a far cry from her usual smooth tones.

"I'm doing great, Patsy. How about you?"

"Fine, fine. Just wonderful."

He glanced at his watch. It was nearly nine here, which made it damn late back in North Carolina.

"I've just been having a glass of your Chardonnay and thinking about you," she said.

"That's nice," he replied since he could hardly say "What the hell is up?" to Patsy.

"In fact, I've been thinking about the fun we had the last time we were at the vineyard with Sarah. You remember Sarah, of course?"

Yeah, with every beat of his heart. "Of course I remember Sarah."

He supposed he should ask the obligatory question of how she was doing, but his heart just wasn't in it. He wanted her miserable, missing him. And more than that, he wanted her here. In his life. In his arms. In his damn bed.

"Well, I had lunch with Sarah yesterday. It had been weeks since I'd seen her."

He knew how that went. He also was catching on to the idea that Patsy wasn't looking for a whole lot of interaction in this conversation.

"She was as lovely as always," Patsy said. "Very busy with the new semester about to start, which I suppose along with the fact that she's pregnant might account for her looking a little peaked."

His heart crashed to a stop and then started rolling at a beat he'd never before experienced. "What?"

"She was a little peaked...you know...pale?"

"Not that. The pregnant thing."

Patsy drew in a sharp breath. "Did I say that?"

"Yes, you did."

"I couldn't have said that. It must be all the wine I've been drinking."

Steve stood and started pacing the length of the room. "I'd bet a case of my new red that you haven't had more than two sips. Now start talking."

"I'm sure I must have been drinking. How else could I let slip something that Sarah made me swear just yesterday I wouldn't tell a soul? At least, I'm sure that's what I plan to tell Sarah."

"She's pregnant?"

"Yes," she replied in her normal voice.

"How pregnant?"

"From what she said, just beginning."

He briefly considered the possibility that someone other than he was the father, then discarded it. They'd used protection, but he knew that the possibility of a slipup existed. And beyond that, he knew that Sarah was faithful to her very core. She was far from the sort to have multiple lovers.

"And I'm the father," he said aloud.

"Of course you are. The only question is what you're going to do about it."

He glanced at his watch again. "Pack."

"Good, because I took the liberty of making a flight reservation for you."

He grinned. "Good thinking."

Now if he could just think of a way to make Sarah love him.

ON THURSDAY MORNING, SARAH sat at her office desk trying to ignore the scent of coffee wafting down the hallway. She needed to focus on the earnest junior in her guest chair telling her why he just had to transfer to the motorsports program.

She paged through the student's paperwork. "It says here, Richard, that this is your fifth change of major, and you're only starting your junior year. That's the reason they're requiring a departmental sign-off, and I can't say I blame them. Microbiology...philosophy...mathematics...political science..."

"And now motorsports management. For real this time."

"I'd like to believe you."

"Look, Professor Stanton, you're last on my list."

"I don't think that's quite the approach you want to take," she said.

"What I mean is that I've tried everyone else, and they won't listen. I know that my transcript is messed up, and I know that I've messed up, but that was because I was listening to everyone else and not to what was in my heart. I don't want to be a lawyer because it will make my dad proud or a math teacher like my mom. I want to be involved in NASCAR. I've loved it since I was a little kid. I can tell you the total number of wins between Dean and Kent Grosso and at what tracks they took place. I can—"

Passion. There was no denying its power. Sarah pulled out her pen. "Richard..."

"No, really." She could see by his anxious expression, he believed she was about to turn him down. "Haven't you ever let other people mess you up?"

More than this young man needed to know. She'd let her earlier experiences color her life for too long. Her father had bolted, Martin had cheated and ex number two had been so verbally abusive that she'd lost more confidence with each cutting word. Patsy had been right. Sarah had run from Steve so that Steve couldn't run from her.

"Come on, Professor Stanton. I'll make you proud. I swear I will."

"Sarah..."

She glanced up from her paperwork to see Steve standing in the doorway.

"Steve?"

"You're surprised?" he asked.

Dread mixed with outright fear hit a little closer to the mark. It was one thing to know that she'd pushed Steve away and another altogether to have him looming in her doorway. And he *was* looming.

Steve gave a nod of greeting to the office's other occupant. "Son, do you think maybe you could come back later? Say, tomorrow."

Richard of the fifth major looked as shell-shocked as Sarah felt. He scrambled to his feet. "Aren't you…"

"Tomorrow, son?"

He nodded blankly. "Uh, sure. You are Steve Clayton, aren't you?"

"I am." He hitched his thumb toward the door. "Now if you don't mind?"

Sarah knew that she should be demanding that Steve wait. She knew she should be on the phone taking off a layer of Patsy Grosso's skin, but it was all she could do to remember how to breathe.

In…

Out…

The stars dancing in front of her eyes began to recede. "Wait," she said.

She quickly signed the form's approval line and tried to hand the papers back to Richard. The student, however, was transfixed. Steve took the file and more directly waved it at him. Richard blinked a few times, stammered his thanks and then backed from the small office.

Steve closed the door. Never had her workspace seemed so small. Sarah could hardly find the air to keep breathing.

"So," Steve said, "do you want to go about this by a circular or direct route?"

Direct meant he'd be gone faster, and her heart broke at the thought, but she didn't have the stamina left to drag this out.

"Direct," she said.

"Good," he said. "Enough time has been wasted."

He seemed so tall and ominous.

"Do you think maybe you could sit down?" she asked.

He did as requested. "Is it true you're pregnant with my child?"

Yes would have been both a reasonable and correct answer, but when she opened her mouth, all that came out was a sob. She covered her mouth with her hand and tried for composure, but there was no regaining it. Sarah nodded her admission, then let the tears win.

"Sorry...I'm so sorry," she managed to choke out between sobs.

"For not telling me immediately? You should be."

"No... For this. I can't..." She grabbed one tissue then another from the box on her desk. "I can't help myself."

"That's a start, I guess," he said. "And I'm sorry that I'm making you cry, but we have to get through this. For starters, you should know that sooner or later, baby or not, I was going to end up at your door, Sarah. I love you."

"You... You..."

"Love you. But I gotta say it's pretty tough to come here and do this after you've apparently decided I'm a disposable dad on top of being a discarded lover. I can find a way to deal with the fact that you don't love me, but I damn well refuse to be pushed from this baby's life. Do you understand that?"

She cried harder. So hard that it wrenched down to the bottom of her empty stomach. Steve was looking rattled, not that she blamed him. She was scaring herself.

"Sarah, honey, can I get you anything?"

She wanted to tell him to go back to that talk of love, but she couldn't do much other than try to catch her breath.

"You've been doing a lot of this?" Steve asked.

She managed a frantic nod.

"Look, I realize there's a very good chance that you're going to tell me to go away. That's your right, and if it's what you want, we can work this out between our lawyers."

"No lawyers," she said. "No damn lawyers."

She wrapped her arms around her head and put her face down on the desk as she had during quiet time back in grade school. If ever she'd needed a quiet time, it was now.

A hand settled on her head, and she swore she could feel the love flow right through her to her heart.

"It's going to be okay," he said. "No matter what, I promise you that."

She rested a moment more, letting his calm seep into her. When she lifted her head, she saw him standing next to her. The concern on his face made her certain that she had to let go of the ghosts of her past and face her future, no matter what it might hold.

"You don't want more children," she said. "I've heard you say it more than once."

"When?" He looked genuinely confused.

"When you've been talking with Mattie about her childhood."

"That stuff? I was just joking. Mattie and I always fire back and forth that way."

"There's usually a truth of some sort behind a joke."

"Now you're sounding like your mother."

She considered the thought. "Maybe, but Mom's pretty sharp."

He sat again and expelled a deep breath, as though she'd taken the fight out of him.

"Look," he said, "I know my relationship with Mattie has always been a little bit off. I love her like crazy, but I wasn't the greatest dad to her...too busy, too distracted, too whatever. She got into the habit of goading me to get my attention. She still does it, and I still shoot back without thinking."

"Okay. I can understand those patterns." She'd had her own built-in defenses for a very long time, too. "But you have to understand how they make me doubt you're up for fatherhood."

He paused before speaking, and Sarah appreciated the care he was putting into his thoughts.

"Until Patsy called me, I'd never considered another round of parenthood as anything more than an abstract concept," he said. "I'm fifty, and busy. Hell, until you, I hadn't even dated anyone seriously for years. But then she told me that you're pregnant...." He shook his head. "In that split second, it all became real. It wasn't about me having a baby with some nameless, faceless woman. It was about *you*.... You and me and this life we've made together."

He leaned forward. "That was it for me. Exactly then I knew I wanted to be a father again, because it's us...*our* baby. I'm older than I was with Mattie, and I like to think I'm smarter, too. I regret the fact that I didn't focus on her as I should have, and I'm thankful that she turned out just fine. This time, though, I'm going to be there. I want it more than I've ever wanted anything, except for you in my life in the first place."

It seemed that epiphanies were abundant. Though he was a smooth man, one well-versed in putting out a good line, sheer instinct told her that he spoke from the heart. And how hers danced with joy.

"You mean this," she said.

"I do."

There were things that Sarah needed to say, too. She would start with the most wonderful truth she owned. "I think you should know that I have illogically and inexplicably fallen in love with you."

He tilted his head and looked at her. "The illogical I can buy in to, but the inexplicable? Give me some credit, okay?"

"All right," she said. "Not so inexplicably."

A smile lifted the corners of his mouth. "Can I have another *I*-word? Irrevocably, maybe?"

"Irrevocably. I like that one." She took another moment to let hope settle into her heart. "I have no idea how to make this work, but now that I've seen you again, I don't think I can let go."

His smile broadened. "There won't be any letting go. Not until I've drawn my last breath. Sure, we're both going to have to make some adjustments. You might have to teach a little less after this year, and I'm going to have to get Damon moving on a faster timetable with Pebble Valley's image campaign since I don't want to be its face any more, but we're going to pull this off. I want that new life…a quieter one…and I need you in it every single day."

Sarah laughed. "Quieter? With a new baby?"

"Okay, so maybe not quieter. How about just a little less complicated?"

She shook her head. "You are a dreamer, Steve Clayton."

"Hell, yes, but I'm also a doer. And this we're going to get done."

He got down on one knee. Sarah did a quick mental check for rising nausea, but there was none. This was the right man, the right place, and the right time.

"Sarah Stanton, will you marry me?"

"Yes," she said, and she knew her life would never be the same again. And Sarah was fine with that. She had developed quite a taste for life on the fast track.

* * * * *

*For more thrill-a-minute romances set against the
exciting backdrop of the NASCAR world, don't miss:
FORCE OF NATURE by Kristina Cook
Available in December*

Celebrate 60 years of pure reading pleasure with Harlequin®!

To commemorate the event, Silhouette Special Edition invites you to Ashley O'Ballivan's bed-and-breakfast in the small town of Stone Creek. The beautiful innkeeper will have her hands full caring for her old flame Jack McCall. He's on the run and recovering from a mysterious illness, but that won't stop him from trying to win Ashley back.

Enjoy an exclusive glimpse of Linda Lael Miller's
AT HOME IN STONE CREEK
Available in November 2009 from
Silhouette Special Edition®

The helicopter swung abruptly sideways in a dizzying arch, setting Jack McCall's fever-ravaged brain spinning.

His friend's voice sounded tinny, coming through the earphones. "You belong in a hospital," he said. "Not some backwater bed-and-breakfast."

All Jack really knew about the virus raging through his system was that it wasn't contagious, and there was no known treatment for it besides a lot of rest and quiet. "I don't like hospitals," he responded, hoping he sounded like his normal self. "They're full of sick people."

Vince Griffin chuckled but it was a dry sound, rough at the edges. "What's in Stone Creek, Arizona?" he asked. "Besides a whole lot of nothin'?"

Ashley O'Ballivan was in Stone Creek, and she was a whole lot of somethin', but Jack had neither the strength nor the inclination to explain. After the way he'd ducked out six months before, he didn't expect a welcome, knew he didn't deserve one. But Ashley, being Ashley, would take him in whatever her misgivings.

He had to get to Ashley; he'd be all right.

He closed his eyes, letting the fever swallow him.

There was no telling how much time had passed when he became aware of the chopper blades slowing overhead. Dimly, he saw the private ambulance waiting on the airfield outside of Stone Creek; it seemed that twilight had descended.

Jack sighed with relief. His clothes felt clammy against his flesh. His teeth began to chatter as two figures unloaded a gurney from the back of the ambulance and waited for the blades to stop.

"Great," Vince remarked, unsnapping his seat belt. "Those two look like volunteers, not real EMTs."

The chopper bounced sickeningly on its runners, and Vince, with a shake of his head, pushed open his door and jumped to the ground, head down.

Jack waited, wondering if he'd be able to stand on his own. After fumbling unsuccessfully with the buckle on his seat belt, he decided not.

When it was safe the EMTs approached, following Vince, who opened Jack's door.

His old friend Tanner Quinn stepped around Vince, his grin not quite reaching his eyes.

"You look like hell warmed over," he told Jack cheerfully.

"Since when are you an EMT?" Jack retorted.

Tanner reached in, wedged a shoulder under Jack's right arm and hauled him out of the chopper. His knees immediately buckled, and Vince stepped up, supporting him on the other side.

"In a place like Stone Creek," Tanner replied, "everybody helps out."

They reached the wheeled gurney, and Jack found himself on his back.

Tanner and the second man strapped him down, a process that brought back a few bad memories.

"Is there even a hospital in this place?" Vince asked irritably from somewhere in the night.

"There's a pretty good clinic over in Indian Rock," Tanner answered easily, "and it isn't far to Flagstaff." He paused to help his buddy hoist Jack and the gurney into the back of the ambulance. "You're in good hands, Jack. My wife is the best veterinarian in the state."

Jack laughed raggedly at that.

Vince muttered a curse.

Tanner climbed into the back beside him, perched on some kind of fold-down seat. The other man shut the doors.

"You in any pain?" Tanner said as his partner climbed into the driver's seat and started the engine.

"No." Jack looked up at his oldest and closest friend and wished he'd listened to Vince. Ever since he'd come down with the virus—a week after snatching a five-year-old girl back from her non-custodial parent, a small-time Colombian drug dealer—he hadn't been able to think about anyone or anything but Ashley. When he *could* think, anyway.

Now, in one of the first clearheaded moments he'd experienced since checking himself out of Bethesda the day before, he realized he might be making a major mistake. Not by facing Ashley—he owed her that much and a lot more. No, he could be putting her in danger, putting Tanner and his daughter and his pregnant wife in danger, too.

"I shouldn't have come here," he said, keeping his voice low.

Tanner shook his head, his jaw clamped down hard as though he was irritated by Jack's statement.

"This is where you belong," Tanner insisted. "If you'd had sense enough to know that six months ago, old buddy, when you bailed on Ashley without so much as a fare-thee-well, you wouldn't be in this mess."

Ashley. The name had run through his mind a million times in those six months, but hearing somebody say it out loud was like having a fist close around his insides and squeeze hard.

Jack couldn't speak.

Tanner didn't press for further conversation.

The ambulance bumped over country roads, finally hitting smooth blacktop.

"Here we are," Tanner said. "Ashley's place."

* * * * *

*Will Jack be able to patch things up with Ashley,
or will his past put the woman he loves in harm's way?*

Find out in
AT HOME IN STONE CREEK
*by Linda Lael Miller
Available November 2009 from
Silhouette Special Edition®*

REQUEST YOUR FREE BOOKS!

2 FREE NOVELS PLUS 2 FREE GIFTS!

Silhouette®

SPECIAL EDITION®

Life, Love and Family!

YES! Please send me 2 FREE Silhouette Special Edition® novels and my 2 FREE gifts (gifts are worth about $10). After receiving them, if I don't wish to receive any more books, I can return the shipping statement marked "cancel." If I don't cancel, I will receive 6 brand-new novels every month and be billed just $4.24 per book in the U.S. or $4.99 per book in Canada. That's a savings of at least 15% off the cover price! It's quite a bargain! Shipping and handling is just 50¢ per book.* I understand that accepting the 2 free books and gifts places me under no obligation to buy anything. I can always return a shipment and cancel at any time. Even if I never buy another book from Silhouette, the two free books and gifts are mine to keep forever.

235 SDN EYN4   335 SDN EYPG

Name	(PLEASE PRINT)

Address	Apt. #

City	State/Prov.	Zip/Postal Code

Signature (if under 18, a parent or guardian must sign)

Mail to the Silhouette Reader Service:
IN U.S.A.: P.O. Box 1867, Buffalo, NY 14240-1867
IN CANADA: P.O. Box 609, Fort Erie, Ontario L2A 5X3

Not valid to current subscribers of Silhouette Special Edition books.

Want to try two free books from another line?
Call 1-800-873-8635 or visit www.morefreebooks.com.

* Terms and prices subject to change without notice. Prices do not include applicable taxes. Sales tax applicable in N.Y. Canadian residents will be charged applicable provincial taxes and GST. Offer not valid in Quebec. This offer is limited to one order per household. All orders subject to approval. Credit or debit balances in a customer's account(s) may be offset by any other outstanding balance owed by or to the customer. Please allow 4 to 6 weeks for delivery. Offer available while quantities last.

Your Privacy: Silhouette is committed to protecting your privacy. Our Privacy Policy is available online at www.eHarlequin.com or upon request from the Reader Service. From time to time we make our lists of customers available to reputable third parties who may have a product or service of interest to you. If you would prefer we not share your name and address, please check here.

SSE09R

Love Inspired®

HEARTWARMING INSPIRATIONAL ROMANCE

Get more of the heartwarming
inspirational romance stories that
you love and cherish, beginning
in July with SIX NEW titles,
available every month from
the Love Inspired® line.

Also look for our other
Love Inspired® genres, including:

Love Inspired® Suspense:
Enjoy four contemporary tales of intrigue
and romance every month.

Love Inspired® Historical:
Travel to a different time with two powerful
and engaging stories of romance, adventure
and faith every month.

Love Inspired.
HISTORICAL
INSPIRATIONAL HISTORICAL ROMANCE

He won his fame and freedom in the gory pits of Rome's Colosseum, yet the greatest challenge for gladiator Caros Viriathos is the beautiful slave Pelonia Valeria. Should anyone learn she is a Christian, Pelonia will be executed. Her secret brings danger to Caros… but she also brings a love like none he's ever known.

Look for
THE GLADIATOR
by
Carla Capshaw

Available November wherever books are sold.

www.SteepleHill.com

Steeple
Hill®

LIH82824